DIRTY PRIEST

SINNERS WELCOME

SAMANTHA BARRETT

DEDICATION

Get on your knees and start praying for forgiveness, I'll make a sinner out of you by the end of this book. You'll break your vow of celibacy and join me on a first-class ride down south when our time's up...

"Mom!" I call out as I stand on the landing at the base of the stairs with water lapping at my ankles. I look around and balk at the sight of the entire downstairs being flooded.

"What's wrong?" she calls back.

I scrunch my face and debate how to respond until I feel a searing heat against my back and gasp. I fight back a shiver at the contact. Hudson has grown bolder since I arrived here two weeks ago.

"I wonder if I could get you to squirt?" I suck in a sharp intake of breath. Hudson is my stepbrother and his comments should make me feel sick, but they don't. I feel a pool of heat brewing low in my belly and try to fight against the sensation.

"Oh, my goodness!" I jolt at the sound of my mom's voice and take a step forward, putting some much needed distance between Hudson and me. I look up at my mom and feel horrible when tears shine in her blue eyes. "Oh lord, how the heck did this happen?" she breathes out as she descends the stairs and passes by me and Hudson.

"I'll turn the water main off," he says. The moment he disappears, I release my breath as my lungs start to burn. I follow after my mom and take in the damage. Just as we near the living room, the floor above caves in. We both scream and scramble out of the way, just as the bathtub from upstairs falls through the ceiling, water gushing everywhere.

I reach for my mom, only to slip and fall, soaking myself from head to toe. The water shuts off a second later, and I sigh in relief. I push to my feet, wanting to curse, but I know my mom will lose her shit. Ever since she found God after meeting Ken, she has changed.

She goes to church every Sunday and spends her free time helping the community. My dad is in the army and was just relocated, so I had to either move to some random country with him, or move in with my mom and stepdad. What I didn't know at the time when I agreed to move here, was that Ken's son would be living here while his apartment was being renovated.

"Oh, Peyton, what are we going to do?" Mom cries as I push to my feet and stare down at my clothes. I cringe at the sight of my white shirt, which is now translucent, and my pink bra shining through like a neon light. "Ken and I can't afford to repair the damage."

"Mom, that's why you have insurance," I supply.

She shakes her head and turns to face me, tears cascading down her pale cheeks. "Insurance won't cover this."

I reel back. "Why the hell not?"

Her features tighten. "Language!" I fight back my eye roll and mutter an apology. "They warned us to get the pipes fixed, but we couldn't afford it. Ken has picked up extra shifts at the mill, and I've covered a few of the girls at the diner, but we just..." When her bottom lip begins to tremble, I pull her to me and hug her as she cries. I spot Hudson entering the room over her shoulder. My eyes widen when I notice he's not alone.

The guys with him are just as orgasm inducing as he is. Hudson is hot as sin, with shaggy brown hair that constantly flops onto his forehead and green eyes that sear into you with intensity. The guys that flank him on either side are fucking sinister. They are both shirtless and look like they just rolled out of bed. The one on the left has the body of a gym junkie, his muscles are defined and ripple like a wave, his black hair is cropped short on the top and shaved on the sides, and his brown eyes draw you in like quicksand. But the one on his other side has tattoos across his chest and full sleeves down both arms. His black hair is long enough for you to run your fingers through and tug on the strands. But those eyes, God they are the brightest blue I have ever seen. The sight of Rosary beads around his neck has my brows bunching.

Hudson smirks as if he knows where my thoughts have gone. I blush and pull back from Mom, flicking my gaze over her shoulder. She whirls around and gasps. "Oh, Father," Mom weeps and rushes toward the tattooed bad boy. He wraps his arms around her, and she begins blabbering on about what happened while I stand here with wide eyes and my mouth ajar. Hudson chuckles and stalks toward me, with the other guy following him.

"Peyton, meet Kye, our neighbor."

I splutter. "You're our neighbor?" I squeak out, then shoot Hudson a glare when he laughs. Kye smiles, and fuck me if it doesn't do things to my insides.

"Yeah, nice to meet you, " he rasps out. Before I can respond, the tattoo stranger snags my attention when he speaks.

"We'll organize a fundraiser. The church will do what it can to help your family, Lenior." I snap my gaze to Hudson in question. The asshole just grins and bends down until his lips brush against my ear, sending a shiver down my spine.

"I told you to come to church on Sunday," he whispers.

"Why?" I ask breathlessly.

"Meet our Priest, Father Pierce." My eyes widen to the size of dinner plates as I gawk at the priest. His gaze is locked onto mine as my mother continues to spew her problems.

How the hell can this guy be a priest when he oozes devilish vibes?

"Peyton!" My mother snaps as she whirls around, scowling at me. I scrunch my face in confusion.

I suck in a sharp breath when Kye brushes up against my side and says low enough for only me to hear. "You said that out loud, Bunny."

Shame washes over me. I feel heat staining my cheeks. "Sorry, Father," I mutter and cringe when the priest smirks at me.

"Don't be. You won't be the first to assume that, and I'm sure you won't be the last. And please, call me Van." If I could get away with face-palming myself without being seen, I would do it.

"What are we going to do?" Mom chokes out.

"You won't be able to stay here," Van says.

"They can stay in my apartment," Hudson offers.

Mom purses her lips and shakes her head. "We can't do that. You only have one room completed. You should stay there."

"Lenior, you and Ken should stay at Hudson's place," Van urges.

"I can't leave Peyton," she shoots back. When Van looks at me, the air rushes from my lungs, and I swear I see a flicker of lust in his eyes when they drop to my chest. I balk when I realize why. I quickly cross my arms over my chest to shield my bra from all of their views.

"Peyton and Hudson are welcome to use the spare

rooms at our house until we can get your house fixed and livable again. I promise we will take *really good* care of your daughter." Call me crazy, but I get a sense that the priest had a hidden meaning in his statement.

Ken arrived home not long after my mom called him. I actually felt really bad for them both. They both work hard and having something like this happen to their home is horrible. Ken felt the same way my mom did. He didn't want to move into his son's place, but Van asked if he would prefer to live with him and Kye. Ken's face said it all, so now I'm left with no option except to move in with the priest and his best friend.

I stand on the pathway out front of their house. Hudson gathered his things and left as quickly as he could to move in next door. I waited until my mom and Ken left to assure her I would be fine living with three guys. I snort. What mother would let her nineteen-year-old daughter move in with three young guys who look like walking panty destroyers?

Mine!

My own mother has just signed me up to be sexually frustrated for the foreseeable future. I packed my rabbit, there was no way I was leaving that behind. I've been on edge all damn day thanks to these three, and I just know seeing them every day is going to be hell.

"You going to stand out here all night or come in?" I screech and jump in fright at the sound of his voice. I place my hand over my chest and look toward the side of the house where I see Van leaning, and to my utter fucking surprise, he's smoking!

"I thought that shit was against the bible or something?" I snark.

He chuckles, then takes another drag of his cigarette. "I won't tell if you don't?"

I roll my lips over my teeth. "Which room is mine?" I ask, changing the subject.

"The third on the right upstairs." I move to take a step, but his confession has me pausing. "Unless you want to hear your brother moaning, I wouldn't go in there." I roll my eyes and ignore the priest, not bothering to unpack the meaning behind that statement. I push the door open, and to my surprise the house is clean. No sign of dirty socks or jocks anywhere. Utterly wrung out after the day from hell, I make my way upstairs and decide to explore my new home tomorrow. I stop at the first room and peer inside the open door. I always thought boys were supposed to be messy, but the bed is made, and everything on top of the dresser is arranged in such a way that leads me to believe everything in here has a place, and every place has a thing, if ya get my drift.

"Fuck!" I jerk in fright and whirl around, trying to find

the source of the sound, but the hallway is empty. Frowning, I move toward my room only to freeze. "Fuck, like that, Kye." My eyes widen when I realize that it's Hudson!

I creep closer to the second door, which is ajar. I know I shouldn't snoop, but I feel compelled to. I peek through the crack, and sweet baby Jesus!

The sight has my jaw hitting the floor and my blood running hot at the sight. "Fucking take it," Kye growls. My heart is beating so loud I fear they might hear it. I almost gasp out loud when my pussy starts to throb and clench on air at the sight of Kye bending Hudson over the edge of the bed, his cock buried deep in his ass. The sight of Kye's muscles flexing as he pounds into my stepbrother causes my mouth to dry. Hudson looking so blissed out and on the verge of ecstasy has me panting.

"Like what you see?" I scream and jump a foot into the fucking air, knocking the door wide open. Kye and Hudson both snap their heads up and look directly at me. I feel Van at my back, and his hot breath hits the back of my neck as he says, "Don't stop on our account." To my utter horror, Kye laughs, and Hudson just smirks as Kye draws back and slams inside, drawing a long groan from my stepbrother.

CHAPTER TWO

HUDSON

I've seen how she has watched me since she arrived. Peyton has no idea how to keep her feelings from being plastered across her face. She wants me. I know it, and so does she, but she is too worried about the taboo aspect of fucking things.

The look on her face last night as she watched Kye fuck me is a sight forever ingrained in my mind. She wanted to appear disgusted and ashamed, but I saw through her bullshit. The subtle way she shifted on the spot and how she rubbed her thighs together gave her away. If it wasn't that, then it sure as fuck was the sight of her nipples poking through her thin crop top. She tried to use her blonde hair as a curtain to shield her face from us, but Van just gripped the strands in his fist and yanked her head back, forcing her blue eyes wider as she was made to watch Kye and me.

Poor little Peyton Jordan has no idea what the fuck she is in for. Knowing she is at our mercy has my cock growing hard, and it isn't even seven in the morning.

"We need to head to the church as I want to get a head start on the fundraiser. The quicker we can get this sorted, the quicker your dad and Lenior can get their house fixed." I take a bite of my toast and look at Van leaning against the counter, sipping his coffee. Van isn't what you would expect a priest to be. He looks nothing like one, either.

"Yeah, I can help with the repairs when I get off work," Kye adds.

I sigh. "I'll shuffle a few of my jobs around. My apartment will have to wait, I guess," I say.

Van scoffs. "Yeah, you seem so distraught about having to live here and having access to Kye whenever you want." I smirk at the prick and wag my brows.

"Like I said, brother, any time you want to join, the door is always open." Kye bursts out laughing, and Van just shoots me a filthy look.

"I'm gonna head out." We all snap our heads toward the entryway to see Peyton standing there. She won't look at any of us. I can see a blush already staining her cheeks, and I fight not to poke fun at her. Last night was a lot for her, no doubt. Once Kye and I finished, Van released her, and she ran to her room—she didn't come out once.

"Where are you going?" I press.

She lifts her head and shoots me the filthiest look I have ever seen. It doesn't have the desired effect she had hoped, though. All that fire in her eyes does is make my dick strain against the zipper of my jeans.

"Out," she bites out and turns on her heel. I slip off my stool and wave goodbye to the guys as I chase after her. I catch up to her just as she steps outside. She whirls around with her fist raised. I pause and dart my gaze between her tiny hand and her face, arching my eyebrow. She growls and drops her fist back to her side. "What do you want?"

I pull the door closed behind me. "Come on, I'll give you a ride into town," I say as I brush past her.

"I have my own car!" she snaps.

"Did you want a round of applause?" I deadpan.

"I'm not going anywhere with you."

"Why, because you saw me with a cock in my ass or because you wished I had mine inside yours?" Her jaw unhinges. Before she can reply, I add, "Get in the car, Peyton. Your mom wants us to meet her at the diner." At the mention of her mom, she snaps her mouth closed and stomps past me to head to my truck. I bite my lip to keep from smiling. Fucking with her has become my new favorite thing because I can see how uptight she gets when it concerns sex. I've heard her on the phone to her friends. I know for certain she's no virgin, and I also heard her tell her friends what she's into sexually.

We've barely turned out of the street when she says, "I won't say anything about what I... walked in on."

I snort out a laugh. "Is that what the cool kids are calling spying these days?"

She scoffs. "I wasn't spying!"

"What were you doing then?" I fire back. I glance her out of the corner of my eye, getting all flustered.

"I... I was trying to find my room and accidentally saw—"

"Kye giving me one of the best orgasms of my life?" She snaps her head toward me so fast I know it had to have hurt.

"Hudson!"

"What?" I say with a shrug.

"That's... no, we shouldn't be talking about this."

"Why not?"

She throws her hands into the air and fuck me, she looks sexy sitting there, getting all hot and bothered. "Because you're my stepbrother, and what you do in your private time is none of my business."

"What if I wanted it to be your business?" She sucks in a sharp intake of breath.

"Don't," she mutters.

"Don't what?" I press.

"Don't do... that!" she hisses, then faces away from me just as we pull up out front of the diner. We live in a small town, and everyone knows everyone here. The joys of living in a country town in the middle of nowhere means you never get to keep a secret for too long. If I wasn't the only builder in town, I would never get any business. Mrs. Jenner saw Kye and I making out behind the church a couple of years back and ran her mouth so fast the whole town knew before the service was over. Ever since that day, most of the town has kept away from us, fearing our bisexuality would rub off on them somehow.

The second I put the truck in park, Peyton jumps out and rushes inside. I can't help but laugh. She can try and appear unaffected by what she saw last night, but Kye and I both heard her moaning through the thin walls. She was getting herself off to images of us. I push those thoughts away as I follow after her. Lenior is behind the counter, serving Fred and Barney their breakfast. She smiles at me and motions for me to join Peyton down at the end. I do as I'm told. Peyton stiffens when my thigh brushes against her leg.

To distract her, I ask, "Have you always been into primal play?" She swivels around on the stool so fast she nearly topples over. I reach out and grip her waist to steady her. Her gaze bores into mine, and for a split second, I see the need burning in the depths of her eyes before the look vanishes when she blinks.

She bats my hand away, steadies herself on her seat, then looks around to make sure no one is listening. Aside from us, there are four people here, and two of those people are her mother and the cook.

"I don't know what the hell you are talking about," she hisses.

I purse my lips and raise my hands as if surrendering. "You know the walls are just as thin at my dad's as they are at Van and Kye's." It takes my meaning three seconds to sink before her eyes are wide and her cheeks turn red. "Next time you want to get off, come knock on my door. I'd be all too happy to get on my knees for you, Pey. Or, if you like, I can chase you through the woods out back to embrace that kink of yours you told your friends about last week."

"Sorry to keep you both waiting." I turn toward Lenior and smile, distracting her while Peyton gathers herself.

"Don't be. We were just discussing what we wanted to *eat*." A strangled sound escapes Peyton, and it takes a fuck load of effort to keep my face blank.

"I can whip you both up something quickly before you head down to the church to meet the others."

"What?" Lenior faces Peyton and purses her lips.

"Didn't Father Pierce tell you?"

Pey looks from her mom to me, then back again when I give nothing away. "No, he didn't mention anything last night... I went to bed early." I bite the inside of my cheek to keep from grinning like a fool.

"Oh, well, he has been so kind and offered the church's help in fundraising. This year's Easter parade proceeds will go toward fixing our house, so I told him you would both go down and lend a hand."

"Mom! I have plans," Peyton rebukes.

"What plans?" I press, earning a glare from the angry little rabbit.

"None that concern you," she forces out through clenched teeth.

"Pity, Kye and I would have loved to *come* along and hang out." Her eyes widen slightly before she schools her features.

"Peyton, please. I don't get off until later, and Ken is working a double shift at the mill. We could really use your help."

Guilt churns in her blue eyes. "Yeah, okay, Mom," she relents.

Oh, sweet little bunny, corrupting you is going to be so much fun.

CHAPTER THREE

PEYTON

Being new to town sucks!

Every person who has come to the church to offer their help has made a big deal about meeting me. I'm so sick of fake smiling and trying to act like a God-loving girl like they expect because of who my mother is. I have nothing against God himself or anyone who goes to church. My dad just raised me differently is all. I was raised to believe that I should be able to choose my own path and not have it forced upon me. Mom has never done that intentionally. My parents are amazing, and Ken is a great guy. I just didn't expect to live in this town. I visited once a few years ago after Mom and Ken got married, and that was enough for me. But now, I find myself calling this place home for the next two years until my dad is stateside again.

I growl when more paint splatters on my shorts and stomach. "This is bullshit," I snarl.

"Cursing in the Lord's house is a no, no." I whirl around to see a raven-haired girl with a pixie cut standing behind me, smiling. Her green eyes are filled with mischief. Her dress style is so different from everyone else in this town. Like me, she wears cargo pants and a black crop top. She moves toward me and snags one of the spare paintbrushes next to the giant Easter Bunny I am currently painting. "I'm Tess."

"Peyton," I say.

She rolls her eyes and smiles. "I know. You are all everyone in this two-horse town has been talking about since you arrived."

I reel back. "Why?"

"Dude, the second you drove through town when you arrived and all the ladies got a look at how hot you are, they locked their sons indoors and made them read the bible." My eyes jump to my hairline. "I'm not even lying. My mom made my brother pray all night for gawking at you as you drove past." Laughter bursts out of me. I feel bad for laughing, but fuck, that is some backend bullshit right there.

"Wow, that's just... wow," I say through my laughter.

"I know, right? Even though she primps herself up for church every Sunday in the hopes Father Pierce will notice her new pearls." We both break out into fits of laughter, and suddenly my day doesn't seem so dreary. Tess tells me she is taking college classes online like me, as her mother wouldn't let her move four hours away to the closest college. I grunt my agreement. My mom wouldn't allow that either. She thought I would fall into the trap of frat parties and fucking anything with something that *dangled between his legs*—her words, not mine.

By the time we finish painting the Easter Bunny and half of the welcome sign, I'm drenched in sweat. The sun is unforgiving today. I reach up and swipe the sweat from my forehead with the back of my arm.

"Hey, Bunny." I whirl around to see Kye leaning against the side of the church with his large arms crossed over his chest, a shit eating grin on his face. I narrow my eyes at him and he uncrosses his arms then raises them as if surrendering. "I was only checking out your ass for like two point five seconds, I swear." Tess laughs. I shoot her a glare, which has her coughing to mask her laughter. "Sup, Tess," Kye says.

"What's up, Kye."

"Nothing much. I just got off work and thought I should be a decent guy and come rescue you ladies from slave duty." My brows draw in.

"Aren't you supposed to be helping?" I ask.

Kye scoffs. "Ah, no. What the hell gave you that impression?"

"You said you would help with the repairs?"

"Yeah, with your house, not this," he says, motioning toward all the plywood cutouts and paints scattered around the church's front lawn.

"You don't go to church, do you?" I hedge.

Tess snorts. "The closest Kye Huxley has ever been to church is sitting in the back row so he could finger my cousin Sharee."

Kye grins and wags his brows. "Those confession room things come in handy when you need somewhere to fuck." I balk at his crassness.

"You slept with someone in the confessional?" I squeak.

He shrugs. "And?" I open my mouth, but nothing comes out. "How about I steal you both for a couple of hours, and we head to the lake to cool off?" Before I can reject his offer, Tess tosses her brush into the bucket and grabs my hand, dragging me toward Hudson's truck. When she pulls the door open, I yank free of her hold and turn to face Kye.

"Won't Hudson get mad we're taking his truck?"

Kye just laughs and nods. "Oh, for sure. Now hurry up before he catches us and ruins the fun." Suddenly I feel giddy at the prospect of annoying my stepbrother and climb in the middle. Tess scoots in beside me just as Kye climbs behind the wheel. Before he even has a chance to start the truck, Hudson and Van appear in the church doorway, and both frown when they see Tess and I aren't where we are supposed to be. Kye starts the truck and the both of them snap their heads toward the truck. The second their eyes land on me, they jump down the few steps and begin sprinting toward us.

"Go, go, go, go!" I yell as Kye slams the truck in

reverse. Tess begins laughing, and I start to panic. Kye slams the brakes on to shift into drive, but before he can plant his foot on the gas, Van and Hudson both grip the tailgate of the truck and heft themselves into it.

"Oh well, I guess the boys are also coming swimming." Uncontrolled laughter tears out of me. Today has been the most fun I have had in a long time. I peer through the back window to see Van and Hudson each pressed into a back corner with arms spread out on the edge of the bed of the truck, their legs kicked out in front of them. God, they are deadly to look at when they smile. "Hey, Bunny?" I look at Kye, who is grinning at me. "I think you're drooling." Tess cracks up laughing, and I give Kye the bird, then slouch back against my seat, ignoring my new friend and her laughter.

When we arrive at the lake, I slip out of the cab and stuff my hands in my pockets, expecting Hudson to lose his shit over us stealing his truck. When he leaps out of the back and barrels toward me, I brace for him to start yelling, but instead, he slings his sweaty arm over my shoulder and leads me down toward the stunning lake.

"Wow," I breathe out. I've only ever seen places like this in pictures. It's gorgeous.

"Not like the city, huh?" Hud jests. I shake my head as he removes his arm and yanks his shirt over his head. I'm powerless to stop myself from drinking in the sight of his tanned skin glistening in the afternoon sun. His abs flex, and I have to bite back a groan. His green eyes dance with sin as he winks at me when he pushes his basketball shorts down his legs. I turn away, only to be met with the sight of Kye stripping down out of his clothes. I turn again, only to see Van standing there in his briefs, his eyes on me. The sound of Kye, Hudson, and Tess laughing and splashing behind me fades as I get lost in the eyes of the priest.

"I've sinned enough in my life. If I am to sin again, it will be for a sure thing, not for a moment of fun."

"Huh?" I rasp, forcing my eyes to remain on his face and not drop lower.

"Your eyes say what your mouth doesn't. Looking is fine but touching is a new ball game. I wear the white collar because it keeps my urges in check. You don't want to know the person I am when I'm without that collar." Van leaves me standing here, reeling as he runs toward the lake. I nibble on my bottom lip, mulling over his words, trying to decipher his meaning.

"Get your ass in here, Bunny, or I'm throwing you over my shoulder!" I whirl around and shoot Kye the bird, which just makes him laugh.

"Stop calling me that!" I call back.

"But you look like a cute little rabbit," Kye says with a fake pout.

"Oh, she loves her *purple rabbit*." I balk at Hudson, and I grind my teeth when the prick shoots me a wink.

"Come on, Pey," Tess urges.

"I don't have a suit," I say sadly.

"Are you wearing a bra and panties?" Van asks.

Everyone falls silent as they wait for my reply. I can feel Kye and Hudson staring at me as I look at Van.

"Yes," I force out.

Van just shrugs. "Then you have a suit. You've got thirty seconds to get in before we chase you." In unison, the three of them take a step forward, and I quickly reach for the hem of my crop top and pull it over my head. I ignore the feeling of their eyes on me as I pop open the button on my shorts and push them down my legs.

CHAPTER FOUR

KYE

Jesus Christ!

My cock is straining against my boxers at the sight of her in that red bra. When she straightens and I see the bottoms, I bite back a groan. She isn't wearing panties, she's wearing a thong, and now I need to see her from behind. Fuck, her ass looks amazing in those shorts, and I know it will look even better now with that thin scrap of material between her cheeks.

Her full tits bounce as she walks toward the edge of the lake. I spy the guys on either side of me. They're both staring at her with hunger. Peyton has had mine and Van's attention since she moved in next door. I even went to fucking church last Sunday just to catch a glimpse of her, but she never showed. Hudson called me on it the second he saw me sitting in the back. When he told me about overhearing some spicy conversations Peyton was having with her friends, my dick was hard every day just thinking about the deprived things our pretty little bunny wants done to her.

"Stop staring at me!" she hisses as she breaches the water's edge. I shake my head and suddenly remember to swallow. Tired of waiting for her, I rush forward. Her eyes widen in surprise. She attempts to turn and flee, but I capture her around her waist and throw her over my shoulder. She screams, but it's quickly followed by laughter. Her perfect ass is in line with my face, and I'm powerless to curb my desire when I bite the soft flesh of it. She gasps and stiffens in my hold.

"Come on, let's have shoulder wars," Tess calls out. Fuck, I forgot she was here! I walk toward the guys and smirk when I see them trying to adjust themselves discreetly under the water.

"Kye, put me down." Peyton tries to sound angry but fails, and when she begins wiggling, I smack her ass, loving the sound of her gasp. "Don't you fucking spank me!" she scolds.

"Oh, did you just curse in front of a priest?" I tease. Before she can reply, I grip her waist and pull her down my front, making sure she can feel *every* inch of me. Her gaze snaps to mine, and redness begins to bloom in her cheeks. I shoot her a wink and step back.

"Come on, Tess, you're with me. Hudson, you ref the match. Van, you get Bunny." I make quick work of getting Tess on my shoulders. We turn to face Peyton and Van and I fight back a smirk. Van is hanging onto his control by a thread. I just know Peyton is going to be the one to get him to snap, and I'm fucking living for that moment.

"Are you okay with this?" Pey asks Van.

He grunts and nods as he bends down. "Climb on," he grits out. She does as he says, and I'm now instantly jealous of my best friend for having her ass on him. Van looks angry, but I know it has nothing to do with Peyton. It's the war happening inside himself. He thinks his sexual urges are dirty and despicable, hence the white collar he now fucking wears. Growing up with Hudson and me, you would think Van would be used to us not giving a fuck what others think, but it turns out we were wrong, and he just needs to learn to deal with his shit, or he will lead a lonely fucking life. Neither Hudson nor I want that for him.

We spend the next couple of hours at the lake with the girls. It's been fun hanging out with Peyton and getting to know her. It took a while for her to relax enough to talk freely. Initially, my attraction to her was based on sexual urges, but after spending time with her, I've actually enjoyed talking to her and hearing what she has to say.

The drive back to the church isn't filled with the same awkward tension. It's easy, and believe it or not, it's comfortable. We drop Tess at home since Van said to call it a day, as he got some of the others at the church to pack things away. Once Tess vacates the seat, Hudson slips in beside Peyton. To my surprise, Peyton rests her head on his shoulder and closes her eyes.

A part of me doesn't want the drive to end, but as the saying goes, all good things must come to an end. I pull into our driveway and kill the engine, but none of us moves. I look over at Peyton and smile at her sleeping form.

"Word of advice, she's a demon when you wake her," Hudson says. I smirk at the fucker as he slips out and gently lays her down. When he reaches back to lift her and carry her inside, Van pushes him out of the way and gathers Peyton in his arms. Neither of us comments because Van doesn't ever do anything without a reason. Hudson and I follow after Van. He carries her upstairs, and I expect him to take her to her room, but he veers and heads for the bathroom. Like moths to a flame, Hudson and I trail after him.

He maneuvers her in his hold and gently rests her ass on the edge of the counter, situating himself between her legs. Peyton stirs and slowly blinks her eyes open. It takes her a second to take in her surroundings, then, when she sees Van between her legs, she tenses.

"What are you doing?" she whispers.

"Helping you. Now, do you need help, or can you shower yourself while I cook, and those two go pick up my car?" She nibbles on her bottom lip and shakes her head.

"I don't need help."

Pity.

Van nods and steps back. Hudson closes the bathroom door when Van steps out. The three of us head downstairs and into the kitchen, where Van begins grabbing what he needs for dinner from the fridge.

"She's stuck in her own head," Hudson announces.

"She doesn't even know us," Van rasps out as he starts chopping some tomatoes for the salad he's making.

"She doesn't need to. She just needs to let us in, and the knowing part can come later," Hud defends.

Van shakes his head. "A girl like *her* doesn't let three random guys get within six feet of her—"

I cut him off before he can continue. "She let me bite her ass."

Both of them roll their eyes, and Hudson focuses on Van as he says, "You think she isn't into randoms, is that it?"

"No, she would rather us be randoms. The fact you are her stepbrother, Kye is her neighbor, and I'm the fucking town priest makes shit complicated, Hudson. Don't you see that?" I smirk so wide my cheeks begin to ache. "Why are you grinning like an idiot?"

"You said *three, us* and not just you two! You like her, don't you?" Van grinds his teeth so hard I think he may break them.

Before Van can reply, Hudson cuts in. "Fine, the fundraiser is when we will do it. For the next week, we keep edging her, and then, on the night of the fundraiser, we give in to two of her wants." The devilish look in his eyes sparks something inside me.

"What did you have in mind?" I hedge.

"We chase her with masks on. She'll give in because she'll be so desperate for release after a week of us taunting her."

"I like it!" I confess.

"You in?" Hud asks Van.

"I took a vow—"

"You wouldn't be breaking that vow. When you put that mask on, you will no longer be Van Pierce. You'll just be some guy chasing a girl through the woods and fucking her brains out." Hudson sounds like a fucking creep.

Van looks between both of us with a stern look. "This happens once, and then we never speak about it again."

"Deal," both Hudson and I agree.

CHAPTER FIVE

PEYTON

For the past week, I have tried to spend as little time as possible at home. It's almost as if Van, Kye, and Hudson are trying to drive me out of my mind. I've spent every day at the church helping out as per my mother's request. This is not how I had planned to spend my break before starting college, but each afternoon, the guys take me to the lake, and I admit that I enjoy hanging out with them. Kye is funny and always finds the light in a dark situation. Hudson is still a dirty flirt and says the most inappropriate things, but he's grown on me... a lot. Van, oh sweet, tortured Van. He is the hardest of the three to get a read on. He doesn't smile freely like Kye, he isn't handsy like Hudson, but he is the best at giving smoldering looks that set my blood pumping and my heart racing.

If this wasn't a small town and they weren't who they were, I would give in to my need. Hudson and Kye have said on numerous occasions this week that they could see us as a foursome. At first, I just laughed and brushed it off, but after the third day, I started to feel like they actually meant it.

Every night, I have heard Kye and Hudson fucking, and it's driving me insane, picturing them and how hot it was to see them together the night I first moved in. Seeing Kye's powerful body thrust inside Hudson has plagued me. Watching Hudson grip the sheets, the look of pure exhilaration on his face was euphoric.

I want to see it again.

I'm lying here staring up at the ceiling, trying to ignore the sounds coming from the next room. I wish I could find my rabbit, but it's grown fucking legs and taken off some-where. I accused Hudson of stealing it, but he swore it wasn't him. I'm itching to run my fingers through my slick folds and get myself off, but I'm never quiet when I come, and I don't want Kye and Hudson to know I'm getting off to them, so I creep out of my bed and head downstairs.

I halt at the edge of the living room when I see Van sitting there with a cigarette hanging out of his mouth. He flicks his gaze to me and nods to the seat beside him. I take it without thought and huff in annoyance. I've been on edge all fucking week, and it's because of these three sex symbols walking around shirtless. Kye has been helping Hudson work on my mom and Ken's house every day after we get back from the lake. It turns out that Kye owns the local mechanic shop, and Hudson owns his own contracting company, so he's able to help with the rebuild next door.

We need the money for the plumbing, which is where Van comes in to save the day.

"Do you think we'll raise enough tomorrow night?" I ask, then cringe when we hear the headboard slam against the wall upstairs. Van turns the volume on the TV up and butts out his smoke in the ashtray beside him. I still find it weird that he's a Godly man, but smokes and curses. He told me no one in town knows about his slip-ups.

"Eager to get out of here?" he says, bringing a frown to my face.

"No, why would you say that?" I find myself asking. He reaches out and tucks a stray hair behind my ear but doesn't remove his hand from my face. My breath hitches, and my core clenches. I'm already turned on from listening to Kye and Hudson, and now having Van touch me so intimately is causing my hormones to go haywire.

"You should want to leave here," he says quietly.

"Why?" I whisper as he leans in until his face is an inch away from my own.

His eyes darken and drop to my mouth as he speaks. "If only you knew the ungodly things I want to do to you." My mouth parts in a silent gasp, and before I can respond, his lips are on mine. When his tongue forces its way inside my mouth, a heady moan escapes me. I wrap my arms around his neck and pull him closer. I can taste the smoke on him, which would normally disgust me, but it just adds to the allure of Van. He grips the back of my neck and uses his body to force me back until I'm lying flat on the sofa, never breaking the kiss.

His free hand skates down my body, and I'm on fire just from the kiss, but the moment he pushes his hand inside my sleep shorts, I overheat. He pushes my panties to the side and glides a finger through my slick folds. He growls his approval when he feels how wet I am.

Breaking the kiss, he asks, "Is this for me or for them?"

I hold his gaze as I answer, "Both." He hums his approval, then kisses me again, robbing me of air when he pushes that finger inside my wet pussy. I arch off the couch, crying out, but he swallows the sound. I open my legs as wide as I can, needing this release so fucking badly. Van is an expert and doesn't need directions. He hooks his finger at the perfect angle and strokes that sweet spot inside me over and over again, bringing me to the edge, only to stop. When he does it a third time, I break the kiss and glare up at him to find him smiling down at me. "Stop playing with me and make me come," I force out through clenched teeth.

Van withdraws his finger and holds it between us. I can see my arousal glistening on it from the light of the TV. Van presses it against my lips. "Suck it." Like a puppet obeying its master, I open for him and moan at the taste of myself. Van yanks his finger out and then replaces it with his tongue. He groans, and that sound sends shivers down my spine and my need for release soars to new heights.

"Nice to see we weren't the only ones getting off." Van breaks our kiss at the sound of Hudson's voice and doesn't move even when I push against his chest. He peers over his shoulder at Hudson and Kye with a triumphant grin and says.

"She tastes so much sweeter than she looks." I balk.

"Fuck, now I'm hard again," Kye whines. I bury my face in Van's chest, trying to hide.

"I want a taste," Hudson says. My brows leap to my hairline.

"God, save me," I mumble against his chest.

Van snorts. "Let's not bring the big man into this. He doesn't need to see his priest defiling one of his subjects."

The shame is fucking real right now!

I woke up earlier than the others in the morning and slipped out of the house before they stirred. There is no way I could face them after last night. I went to bed hot and bothered and barely slept a wink, thanks to Hudson and Kye going at it again! Van's lucky his room is at the other end of the hallway. I nearly died when I heard Kye come, groaning *my* name!

God, I let a fucking priest finger me on the sofa!

I've never been ashamed of my sexuality and the things I want to explore. My dad has always been open about sex and made sure I was protected when I told him I wanted to get rid of my V card. My mom, on the other hand, thinks sex before marriage is a sin. That's rich coming from her since she was pregnant with me before she married my dad. I believe in trying before buying, if ya catch my drift.

But, when it concerns Kye, Hudson, and Van, I don't see reason. They aren't like the boys at my old college. They aren't even boys. They are men—gods if you will. I've seen how all the women in this town look at them, undressing them with their God-loving eyes, and if that makes them a sinner, what the fuck am I since I allowed their priest to slide his fingers inside my dripping cunt? To make everything worse, I woke up with my period, so there will be no action for me for the time being.

I force those thoughts away as I pull into the church parking lot. The fundraiser isn't until tonight, but I know there is still so much to do, so I told my mom I would come down early and help out since she and Ken are both working. Tess offered to help me, and honestly, I could use some girl time right now. Being surrounded by males daily is wearing me down. I know it's wrong to lust after all three of them—

"Argh, get your head in the game, Peyton!" I scold myself before climbing out of the car. I make quick work of gathering the supplies I need to hang the streamers and everything else. Then, I dive into work to distract myself from all thoughts of the guys. When Tess arrives, we finish setting everything up. We move on to the folding table to set up, and once that is complete, I realize we still have the giant Easter Bunny I painted to move out onto the church's front lawn. Tess and I try lifting it, but it's too heavy.

"We need to ask Father Pierce if he can help." I shoot Tess a pleading look.

"Surely there has to be another way—"

Before I can finish, I'm cut off. "I don't mind helping." I peer over my shoulder to see the man himself standing there in his black robe. The white collar I spot has me wanting to cringe, but I don't. The sight of the Bible in his right hand almost has me weeping.

How can he hold that holy book with the same fingers he had inside me last night?

"Thank you!" Tess exclaims and steps back. Van hands his Bible to Tess. I'm about to turn away, but I balk when Hudson ambles around the corner.

"Why aren't you at work?" I hiss.

Hud just winks at me. "I couldn't leave my little sister to do all the *hard* work on her own now, could I?" I swallow and shoot him a scowl when he brushes past me. To my horror, Van unclasps his robe and hands it to Tess. He's wearing a wife beater, which showcases the ink that covers his body, and oh boy, that sight alone has me soaking my panties. As if Hudson can read where my thoughts have gone, he shoots me a wink and a smirk as they pass by with the cutout. I bite back a groan. Those boys will be the death of me and my libido.

"Oh, for the love of all that is holy," Tess mumbles. I stare at my friend with a raised brow.

"What is it?" I ask as I move to her side and follow her stare. A woman, who is clearly in her late fifties, is wearing a low-cut top that exposes her... well-used *tits*. Her face is caked in makeup, and she dresses like a teenager in clothes that aren't her size—*mutton dressed as lamb*. I almost feel sorry for her until she places her hand on Van's chest.

"Who the hell is that?" I snarl.

"That is Annika Pryntz, the town bike." I snap my head at Tess, scrunching my face.

"The town what now?"

Tess rolls her eyes. "Every single man, or married man who wants a bit of fun that isn't his wife, visits Annika. She has been after Van since he took over the church."

Disgust rolls through me as I watch Van take a step back out of her reach. I give her credit, though—she's bold. She closes the space between them, and before she can put her filthy hand on him again, I stalk across the yard and stand in front of Van with a broad smile on my face. Annika sneers at me, but I don't let my smile fall.

"Hi, I'm Peyton."

"If you don't mind, I was speaking to Father Pierce," she says in a clipped tone.

I fake embarrassment. "Oh, I'm sorry. Father Pierce

and my brother are *really* busy setting up for the fundraiser tonight. If you come back later, I'm sure he will make time for you." She opens her mouth to reply, but I turn my back to her and find both Hudson and Van trying their hardest not to laugh. "Don't you boys have work to do?" I snap, then brush past them. I ignore their laughter as I grab Tess's hand and lead her inside the church.

Forgive me, Father. Grant me the strength to fight this pull toward her. I have been trying to resist the urges daily, but they have only grown stronger. I'm weak and need your strength to help me fight it.

"Yo, are you coming?" I sigh and open my eyes. I look to the end of the pew to see Hud and Kye standing there, looking at me expectantly. I wait a minute for a sign or something to tell me that what we are about to do is wrong. When I don't get a single feeling or some gush of wind, I reach up and remove my collar.

"Let's go hunting," I growl. Both my boys' grins mirror my own. We head to the back of the church to my office, where we all change into plain clothes. Hudson reaches into his duffle bag and hands each of us a mask. I hold it in my hands and stare down at it.

It looks like an aged, decrepit rabbit, something out of

a vintage horror film. "I painted them with neon paint." Hudson sounds so proud of himself.

"Why?" I ask as I lift my gaze from the nightmare inducing mask and look at him.

He wags his brows. "Only one of us will chase her to the woods. When we step out of the shadows and she sees the masks, it's gonna send her over the edge and have her primed and ready for us." Excitement runs through me. I've always kept a leash on my sexual cravings because I know they are depraved.

"Why are they rabbit masks?" Kye asks.

Hudson rolls his eyes. "Dude, it's Easter next weekend, so the masks seem fitting. Plus, we all agreed she looks like a lost bunny."

"How are we doing this?" Kye voices. Hudson opens his mouth, but I answer before he can.

"Everyone's leaving. We wait until she finishes packing up, and then we make our move." The idiots high five each other and laugh, making the tension in the room lift. Though, if sexual tension had a scent, it would be wafting through this room right now.

There's a chill in the air tonight. It almost feels like a warning—a sign. I've debated if I should listen and pull the plug on this whole thing, but when the lights in the church flick off, I know I have seconds before she comes out the back to head to her car. Everyone has gone home. Hudson told Peyton we would come down tomorrow and clean up, so she thinks we all went home.

The instant she steps out the back door, the decision is made for me. That white sundress she wears has had me going out of my mind all night. It's a simple halter style dress, but the swell of her tits were visible, and the urge to sink my teeth into them was compelling. Her blonde hair is loose and flows down her back. I've envisioned gripping the strands and wrapping them around my fist as I slam inside her from behind all night long. I've been sporting a hard-on since she put Annika in her place earlier. That woman has been trying to get me in her bed for longer than I care to admit. I may be a priest with wicked and unholy desires, but even I draw the line at touching her. Half the town has been inside her and have used her pussy like the local dumping station.

Peyton turns and descends the stairs. I wait until the last second before I step out of the shadows. A shrill scream of fright escapes her as she stares at me with wide eyes filled with fear.

"Get the hell away from me, or I'll scream." She tries to sound strong, but the tremble in her voice gives away her fear.

I alter my voice as best as I can. "Run."

She jerks back a step. "W-what?"

I take a step forward, and she backs up. "Run. You

have till the count of ten before I start chasing." Her mouth parts in a silent gasp. She tries to head for her car, but I veer before her, cutting off her escape. Panic fills her features as she darts her gaze around. "Seven... six..." She spins around and runs toward the woods like we had planned. I smile behind the plastic rabbit mask, my cock straining against the zipper of my jeans as I give chase.

I can hear her footfalls ahead of me. I slow my pace when I spot her white dress up ahead. "Help!" she calls out. I shake my head. Stupid girl, no one will hear her out here, no houses surround the back of the church—she's at our mercy to do with as we please. "Help!"

She comes to a stop in a small clearing, darting her gaze left and right to try and find a way out. I step into the clearing, forcing her to whirl around and face me. She takes two steps back, shaking her head.

"Here, take them!" she shouts as she tosses her car keys at my feet. A dark chuckle escapes me, causing her brows to bunch.

"Oh, it's not your car *we're* after."

"What do you want?" she snaps, her head raised in defiance.

"You." I couldn't have planned the boys' timing better myself. Kye appears on her right, and his mask glows in the shadows. She starts trembling at the sight of him. When she spins to her left, ready to run, she freezes at the sight of Hudson, standing there with his mask glowing bright. She looks between the three of us before focusing her attention back on me.

"I don't have any money," she pleads.

Hudson and Kye both chuckle. I'm over words, so I move toward her. She retreats until she slams into a tree, and then a whimper escapes her when I crowd her space. Her bottom lip begins to tremble as I reach out and grip the back of her neck, forcing her onto her tiptoes. Her eyes dart side to side as Kye and Hudson flank me.

"Please don't kill me," she begs.

"The only thing we are slaughtering, is that pussy," Hudson says in a voice that sounds nothing like him. Her eyes widen, but this time, it's not with fear. Lust lurks in the depths of those blue eyes. She tries to appear repulsed by the idea and shakes her head as much as she can with my grip on her.

"I... No—" She clamps her mouth closed when I spin her around, turning her face at the last second, her cheek pressing against the bark of the tree. When I trail my free hand down her body and grip her ass roughly, she whimpers. "P-please."

"Please, what?" I snarl. My voice is filled with need. "Eat this pussy?" She whimpers and tries to get free, so I tighten my hold on the back of her neck.

"Who the hell are you?" she screams.

"The guys who are about to embrace the dark, depraved kinks you have always wanted to explore," Kye growls. I nod my head for Hudson to replace my hold. I snatch the rosary beads from my pocket, grab her arms, and bind her wrists, ignoring her pleas. They are half-assed at best, anyway.

"Next time, I'm going to wrap these around my cock and then fuck you with them," I vow. It may be dark, but I can see the flush coating her perfect creamy skin. I glide my hands down her body, not missing the shiver that runs down her spine—her mouth says no, but her body is begging for us to dominate every inch of her.

I grip the hem of her dress and pull it up. The soft glow of the moon allows enough light through the canopy of trees—our masks helping as well—to display her perfect ass. The sight of the scrap of material between her cheeks has a groan escaping the three of us. Kye grabs the bunched material and holds it as I drop to my knees behind her and massage the globes of her ass in my hands.

"If you really want this to end, tell me to stop now, or I'm going to eat this pussy before we fill every one of your holes with our cocks." My voice is taut with tension. Need is riding me harder than ever before as the cravings I have ignored for far too long rear their heads inside me, begging to be set free.

"I... No..." I withdraw my touch. "I have my period." Shame laces each of her words. I narrow my eyes behind my mask.

"Do you really think a little blood is going to stop me?" I snarl. A soft mewl escapes her when I grip her thong and peel it down her legs. I hand the thin scrap of lace to

Hudson, who groans when he feels how soaked it is. He balls the thong up and stuffs it in her mouth. Kye chuckles. Since meeting Peyton, we have come to learn that she hates being silenced, this is a power move to show her *I* am the one in control. I may answer to a higher power when I'm not wearing this mask, but with it on, I call all the shots, and both my boys know that.

I force her legs apart. She tries to fight me, but it's futile. It astounds me that women get embarrassed over having a period. They need to embrace it because there is nothing more sexy than a woman on her period. I reach up and slide a finger through her folds. She leaps onto her tiptoes and struggles against her restraints. I feel the string of her tampon and slowly tug on it. Peyton tries to protest, but her gag muffles her pleas. Once I free her of it, I toss it over my shoulder and push my mask up.

Hudson takes my cue and holds her face so she can't turn back and see me as I part her cheeks and slide my tongue inside her pussy. She cries out, and I groan at the taste of her blood coating my tongue. The second her taste overwhelms me, I lose control, eating her cunt like a rabid animal relishing in the sounds that escape her.

Forgive me, Father, for I feel no guilt over sinning and claiming this pussy.

"Mmmmh," I whimper around my thong as the one on my right holding my face pulls the front of my dress down and frees my tits. He growls in annoyance when he feels my nipple shield, he tears it off, which pulls a cry from me at the sting. As if he can sense the need for pain rising inside me, he draws his free hand back and slaps my tit. I cry out in time as the other one yanks me back, so my pussy is right on his face. I want to be mortified, knowing he will be covered in my blood, but the sinister bitch inside me loves it.

The one on the left grips the hem of my dress and tears the back open. I gasp as the material hangs around my neck until he undoes the knot at the base of my neck. The white material falls to the ground. He reaches around and cups my other breast. He laughs, and the husky sound sends a thrill through me when he pulls the other nipple shield off.

"These things won't keep us from getting to you, baby," he growls. The husky lilt in his voice has my arousal growing to new heights. I have always had depraved fantasies about being chased and fucked by strangers, but I never thought that it would ever become a reality! He bends down and retrieves my ruined dress from the ground as the other one sucks my clit into his mouth, drawing a loud moan from me.

I'm on fire!

My body is overheating with need. The one on the right twists my nipple between his fingers to the point of pain, but I relish in it. The other continues to tongue fuck my wet cunt like he can't get enough of my pussy. The one on the left gathers the material of my dress and wraps it around my eyes, using it as a blindfold.

Not being able to move, see, or speak brings the pleasure to new heights. I'm bound and at the mercy of these strangers. I should be terrified and crying, begging for them to let me go, but I feel none of that. The fact they gave me the option to stop this before they started put all my worries at ease because I fucking want this. I scream when I feel a wet, hot mouth wrap around my nipple and bite down. I cry out again when I feel a finger begin circling my clit while the other pushes his tongue inside my ass. I've never done anal, and I'll admit it scares the hell out of me that my ass cherry might just get popped tonight.

I feel my orgasm building, and I know without a doubt that this orgasm will rock me to my core, leaving me mindless with need. I've had sex before, but not like this—they were vanilla, missionary, and so boring. I want to be owned, dominated, and used like a dirty fuck toy. These three strangers are giving me everything I have ever dreamed of. The feeling of my nipples being sucked, my clit being stroked, and a tongue penetrating my bloody cunt is what finally pushes me over the edge. I scream so loud around the gag as I come harder than I ever have before. My orgasm tears through me like a volcanic eruption—fire blazes through my veins and scorches me as the waves of pleasure wrack my body. I try to pull away, but the fucker grips my waist tighter and continues to tongue fuck me as the other plays with my clit.

I'm a squirter!

The two guys I slept with were grossed out when they learned that little secret, and I'm worried these three will be the same.

Before I can protest or try to break free of their delicious torture, I explode. I scream so loud my throat goes hoarse as I squirt all over the guy's face.

"Oh, fuck," one growls as I quieten down. All three of them have stopped moving, and shame washes over me.

"Did she just squirt?" another asks. I wish the ground would open up and swallow me whole!

"Fuck yes, she did, and now I want to make her do it again, but on my cock." I gasp in astonishment.

They like it?

My train of thought is cut off when I feel the one behind me stand. "Get her on her knees. And get rid of the gag. I want her mouth around my cock."

The two on either side of me do as they are told. I'm moved a couple of steps before I'm pushed to my knees. The debris bites into my sensitive skin, but the pain is redundant, thanks to the need coursing through me. My restraints and blindfold remain in place as the gag is removed. I suck in a lungful of air the instant I'm freed, then, before I can take another breath, I gag when a cock is shoved inside my mouth.

I try to pull back, but his hand tangles in my hair, holding me in place. I gag. He's too big! "Fuck, untie her hands. She can take all three of us, can't you, baby?" the one with his dick in my mouth coos. When he pulls almost all the way out, I begin to relax. "Suck it while they untie you," he barks. I do as he says and bob my head up and down on him. I moan when the taste of his pre-cum hits the back of my throat. I feel one of the others behind me unbind my wrists, and I want to weep in gratitude. A hand grips both my wrists and raises them. I moan around the cock in my mouth when I wrap my hands around the others' cocks, the sound of their groans filling the woods.

"Suck mine, baby." I pull back and release the one in front of me with a wet pop and turn to take the one on the left into my mouth while stroking the other two. I continue alternating between the three of them, loving the taste of each of them. They are big. I just pray I will get to feel them inside me, my pussy is beginning to clench on air, and I know my inner thighs are coated with blood and arousal.

"Have you ever taken three cocks at once?" one of them asks. I pull back, release the one in my mouth, and shake my head. "Do you want to?"

"Yes," I answer without hesitation.

I gasp when a hand cups my cheek, his touch is so tender and warm. "Good girl." The three of them step back, and I begin to worry that they are going to leave until hands grip me under my arms and pull me to my feet. I don't struggle or fight against his hold. When he leans down and meshes his lips to mine, I gasp in surprise, granting him access. His tongue swipes mine, and I swallow a frown pulling at my brows when I taste the metallic tang of blood. It takes me a second to register why I taste blood.

Oh my God!

He's the one who ate my pussy, and now I'm kissing him with my blood on his tongue. Utterly enthralled in the moment, I throw my arms around his neck and relish in the growl of approval that escapes him. His hard length presses against my naked stomach. I break the kiss when I feel the heat of naked flesh pressed against my back.

My train of thought is distracted when the one in front

of me grips my waist and lifts me. I instinctively lock my legs around his waist. I can feel the head of his cock prodding at my entrance, my breathing turns ragged as he slowly lowers me onto him. I cry out the moment he slips inside me. The burn of him stretching me so perfectly overwhelms me. Sweat begins to coat my skin as I try to adjust to his size as he continues to lower me onto him.

I love that he doesn't stop when he knows it's hurting me, he forces my body to accept his large girth, and I relish in the feeling. The instant he bottoms out inside me, I throw my head back and collide with the shoulder of the one behind me and scream. The sound is cut short when the one behind me captures my lips in a kiss. I suck his tongue and drag my teeth along it, loving the groan that escapes him.

"Hold her ass open," he snarls when I release his tongue. The fact I can't see anything only heightens my pleasure. I moan as my ass is gripped and spread. I tense when I feel fingers circle my muscle wall, they are wet and sticky, so I know they came prepared with lube. When he pushes a finger inside me, I tense.

"Hold onto me," the one in front demands. I do as he says and wrap my arms around his neck. He draws back and slams inside me at the same time the finger presses inside my ass and I cry out. It's a weird feeling, one I have never experienced before, but fuck, when he begins moving that finger in and out of me in sync with the other fucking me, I can't get enough. I need more. As if he can hear my thoughts, he adds a second finger. Sounds escape me that I have never heard before. The third one cups my tits and pinches my nipples, making my pleasure more euphoric. I can feel another orgasm cresting, and I try to latch onto it.

"Don't come. Wait until his cock is in your ass, or it will hurt," the third says. I bite down on my lip and try to fight off my impending release. When the fingers withdraw from my ass, I want to protest, but it dies in my throat when I feel the head of his dick edging inside me. I try not to tense and focus on the feeling of the other moving inside my pussy but the burning sensation pulls my focus as he stretches my asshole. my body trembles with the onslaught of pleasure as the other slowly pushes inside me, and soon enough, I get lost in the pleasure. It's heady and wrong but so fucking perfect at the same time. Three men are worshiping my body and giving me everything I have been too scared to try or even ask for.

"Fuck!" the one behind roars when he is balls deep inside my ass.

"Her pussy is strangling the fuck out of my cock," the other says.

"Oh shit, I'm so full," I moan.

"Next time, you will take the three of us at once," the third guy says. My mouth parts in a silent gasp.

Next time...

This isn't a one-time thing!

"I need to move," the one in front says and draws back,

only to slam inside me again. Having all their hands on me and feeling them inside me, along with the heat of their skin, sends my head spinning. It's all too much and not enough at the same time. When they begin to move in sync, cries of pleasure continue to pour out of me without consent. They only grow louder as my orgasm rises inside me.

"Oh fuck, I'm gonna come!" the one in front grits out as he slams inside me. I want to plead for him not to come, that I'm not ready yet. Two more thrusts, and I feel him fill me with his cum. "Hold her," he snaps as he steps back. The one behind me grips my legs and holds them open, exposing my pussy to the other two. "Fuck her while I watch."

I feel the third stand in front of me, and I whimper when I feel him slowly push inside my dirty little cunt. "Fuck!" I scream when he slams all the way in. Sweat beads on my brow when they begin to fuck me hard.

"You like that, baby?" one asks.

"Yes," I cry out when his cock strokes that spot inside my pussy.

"We're going to destroy this pussy," another says.

"Yes, ruin it. I want you to fucking destroy it," I plead as I begin to bounce on both their cocks, chasing my own release.

"Fuck, she looks so good riding your cocks." His praise bolsters my confidence and I continue to bounce up and down on their dicks. My orgasm is right there. When they both draw back and thrust inside me at the same time, I detonate, coming so hard. The one in front pulls out, forcing the other to hold me. I scream and squirt all over him before he's shoving his cock back inside me.

"Yes, fuck my cum back inside me," I scream.

"I'm about to come," the guy behind me says. Four thrusts later, and he's filling my ass with his release. I relish the feeling of having two men's cum inside me.

"I'm coming," the one in front yells a moment after, and then I'm filled with all three of their cum. It feels fucking dirty and like absolute perfection.

The only sounds that can be heard is our heavy breathing. I'm wrung out, exhausted, and so well fucked. This night was everything and one I will never forget. They both pull out of me. I wince, but it's a good type of pain. I know I will feel the ghost of them inside me tomorrow. They don't release their hold on me until they are sure I'm steady, then they step back and I instantly feel cold. I feel something pushed against my chest and grasp it between my hands.

"Put that on when we leave." I realize then it must be a shirt or something.

"Tomorrow night, you will meet us here at midnight," another one says.

"Ah, you want to do this again?" I breathe out. The three of them chuckle. I tense when a hand grips the back of my neck and pulls me flush against a naked chest. He bends until his lips brush against the shell of my ear.

"This bloody little cunt belongs to us now. You made a sinner out of me, and I'll continue to sin just so I can taste the blood of Christ from that cunt." My jaw unhinges. He pulls back, then pushes a finger inside my pussy, drawing a sharp cry from me. Before I can question him, he withdraws his finger, then brings that finger to my forehead. I nearly crumble to the forest floor when I realize what he drew on my forehead.

He used my blood to draw a fucking cross!

After we left her standing there with Van's hoodie clutched against her chest, we hid out in the woods, watching her. She tore that blindfold off, and I waited with bated breath to see if she would regret what had just happened. When I saw her smile and bring Van's hoodie to her nose and inhale, I knew she was made for this shit. We watched her pull it over her head and limp out of the woods. The highlight of the night was watching her climb into her car and stare in the rear-view mirror at the cross painted on her forehead.

The three of us stood there, chuckling. We could see her mouth moving and knew she was cussing us out, but we couldn't hear her from where we were.

We raced home before her so we could change, and Van needed to fucking shower. He had her blood all over his face. We heard her pull into the driveway twenty minutes after we got back. The three of us were lounging on the sofa, acting like we were watching some shit on TV. None of us paid her any mind as she snuck in and ran straight upstairs, but we all laughed when we heard the shower start.

This morning, I'm still sporting a semi. All I could think about all night was how fucking good she felt wrapped around my cock. I've thought about fucking her every day since she moved in with us at home. Finally being able to taste her lips and let my hands roam over her soft, creamy flesh had me busting a nut quicker than I wanted. But, the second she squirted all over my cock, I was done for. She soaked my entire front, and smelling her on me last night before I showered had me stroking one out just from the scent of her cum.

Kye sits beside me at the breakfast counter, drinking his protein shake. Being up this early on a Saturday should be a fucking crime, but we need to clean up the mess from the fundraiser before church tomorrow. Van saunters into the kitchen, sporting his fucking bed hair. My brows raise at the sight of the nail marks on his back when he turns to grab a glass from the cabinet. I open my mouth to tell him to put a shirt on before she sees it, but I'm too late. Peyton saunters into the kitchen, wearing Van's fucking hoodie from last night!

Kye chokes on his protein shake. Van spits the orange juice back into his glass, while I just gawk at her. Her hair is in disarray. I drop my eyes to her knees and fight not to smirk at the small scratches I see there from her kneeling on the ground while she sucked our dicks.

"What the hell are you all looking at?" she snaps. Both Kye and Van begin to mutter some bullshit.

I cut them off. "Who'd you fuck to get that?" I say, pointing to her hoodie. Both the guys snap their gazes to me and glare, but I ignore them, keeping my face blank. Peyton's cheeks begin to heat and she tries to act unaffected by my question but fails.

"Mind your own damn business, Hudson!" she hisses, then brushes past Van, who jumps back a step to avoid touching her. When she reaches up on her tiptoes to grab a glass, all three of us shift to get a glimpse of her flawless ass that peeks out beneath the hem of the hoodie. I bite down on my fist to keep from groaning aloud. Living with her and being around her after tasting her is going to be fucking torture. "What time do we have to be at the church?" she asks no one in particular as she fills her glass with water.

"Nine," Van forces out, then drops his glass in the sink and stalks out of the room.

"Get changed, Bunny," Kye says. She whirls around and glares at him.

"Why?"

I roll my eyes. "Unless you want the three of us to be checking out your ass and pussy all day, I'd put some pants on, little sis." Her jaw unhinges. I laugh at the look on her face and stalk out of the room whistling.

All day I have done nothing but think about Peyton and the sounds she made. Every time I look over at her in those tiny denim shorts and teal tube top, my cock leaps to attention. She has had most of the old fuckers in town staring at her ass every time she bent over, and it's taken everything inside me not to break their noses. They claim to love God, and his word is law and all that shit, but it doesn't stop them from being sleazy fucks and checking her out like a piece of meat. I know Kye and Van feel the same way I do. Kye had purposefully shouldered a few of the fuckers when they stared just a little too long.

He and I are the town outcasts, but it's never bothered us. What we do behind closed doors is none of their fucking business. If they want to judge us for exploring our sexuality, then go for it because it won't stop us. We're best friends who like to fuck. That's it, nothing more, nothing less.

"Next one that looks at her, I'm gonna lose it," Kye snarls from beside me. I grunt my agreement. They aren't looking at her because they think she is beautiful, they are undressing her with their eyes and it's fucking sickening.

"You both are gonna finish cleaning up and do nothing." Both Kye and I face Van. He can act like he doesn't care, but I can see it in his eyes. It's bothering him as well.

"Let them look, as we're the ones who get to taste that sweet cunt, not them."

I snort. "What happened to one and done?" I snark.

Van's eyes narrow. He opens his mouth to curse me out but then remembers where we are. I smile at the fucker. "I'll deal with you later," he forces out.

"I've heard that before," Kye mutters. We both laugh at Van's expense and watch him stalk off, sporting a hard-on under those fucking robes. "He's gonna lose that collar for her."

"He's wanted to give it up for a while but never had a reason to."

"Until now."

"Until *her*," I clarify. Kye grunts his agreement, the excitement coursing through me gives a wicked sense of satisfaction at the prospect of what might happen tonight. I can feel in my gut that Peyton will meet us tonight. There is no way she won't show. I could see it in her eyes this morning. She may not know it was us last night, but we left an impression on her that she can't ignore.

The day has dragged on so slowly that it's almost painful. I keep thinking if I check the time on my phone that somehow the day would have passed by quicker, but all I feel is disappointment every time I look. Eagerness rides me harder than a jockey on the last mile of the track.

"Would you stop fucking fidgeting!" Van hisses. I snap my head up and scowl at the bastard.

"Oh, I'm sorry if my being horny distracts you, *Father Pierce*," I mock.

The fucker narrows his eyes at me, and maybe I shouldn't poke fun at him since we're inside the church and hiding out in his office. He reaches up and grips the white collar, tugging it free, then tosses it onto his desk before leaning back in his chair and looking between me and Kye.

"I broke my vows last night," he admits.

"I was joking," I blurt, wishing I could take back my stupid joke.

"That vow is bullshit, you know it, and so does everyone else," Kye adds.

Van scrubs a hand down his face. "I know, but it doesn't change the fact I sinned, and now I am worse than an imposter. I violated one of my subjects, and I can't undo that."

I snort. "Peyton doesn't want to change what happened last night. If she did, there is no way she would have come downstairs this morning wearing *your* hoodie." I can tell Van is fighting not to smirk.

"Are you worried you broke your vow or are you worried you will be a town outcast like me and Hud?" Kye asks. A pang of guilt hits me. It may not bother me or even affect me that the town thinks I'm dirty for fucking my best friend, but I never really stopped to think about how it affects Kye.

"I don't give a shit what any of these small-minded

pricks think, and they aren't the ones I have to answer to when my time is up. It's simpler for you both. You aren't a priest, but I am! All I could think about all day was the taste of her and how fucking incredible it felt to have her pussy wrapped around my cock. I couldn't even focus when Tom came to confession."

"I would have thought finally being able to release some of that pent up tension would have eased your stress," Kye mutters. I shake my head and smack the idiot's chest.

"What he is failing miserably at saying is..." I snark, "He's a priest, and now he's doubting his faith in the man above because his calling is no longer to serve the big man. He just wants to service my spitfire little sister, and now she is all he can think about." I can't keep the smile from my face as I look at Van. "How about we don't wait for midnight and pay little Peyton a visit at home and take your mind off repenting for your sins, brother?"

"Fuck yeah, I'm so down with that plan," Kye agrees.

"Make her run from the house and escape to the woods out the back, and she'll be soaked by the time I catch her and feast on that delicious pussy," Van says with a devious smirk. My cock is painfully pressed against my pants, begging to be let free.

Ready or not, little sinner, we're coming for you.

CHAPTER NINE

PEYTON

"That's great, Mom," I say as I continue to scrub the oven out. I need something to take my mind off the anticipation of tonight and the only way to do that is to clean.

"Father Pierce went above and beyond for us." I roll my eyes and shoot my phone the stink-eye. "I really hope you will join us at church tomorrow, it would mean a lot to me and Ken to have both you and Hudson there with us." I exhale loudly and try to bite back my snarky remark. She thinks the sun rises out of the priest's ass. If only she knew her favorite person had his fingers inside her daughter's pussy, I wonder if she would still think he was Mr. Perfect?

"Mom, you know I have no interest—"

"Peyton, I want you to be there." Her tone leaves no room for argument. I want to roll my eyes again, but what's the point when she can't even see me? Ever since she called me twenty minutes ago she has been trying to convince me to attend church tomorrow. "Please, Pey, this would really mean a lot to me, Ken and Hudson if you were there with us."

I snort. "Trust me, Mom, Hudson won't give a shit if I'm there."

"I really don't like it when you curse," she scolds.

If you don't like cursing, you would have hated what I did last night.

"Sorry," I mutter as I continue to scrub a tough clump of... I don't even know what it is but it's keeping me busy and my mind off my meeting tonight.

"So, you will be there, right?"

I tip my head back and groan up at the ceiling. "Yes. I'll go if you hang up the phone."

Mom squeals like a schoolgirl, which has me wanting to facepalm myself. "Amazing, Hudson will drive." Before I can protest, she ends the call.

"Fuck!" I growl. She ambushed me and now I'm stuck going to church tomorrow morning to praise a God who would lock those pearly gates on me, hand me a first class ticket down south and kick my ass out. I'm not destined to rejoice with the angels, I'm fated to hang out and play poker with the devil, especially after what I did last night.

My train of thought is halted when the lights go out. I purse my lips, tug off the gloves and dump them on the counter as I grab my phone and turn the torch on. I was raised by my dad so I'm not stupid, I know how to fix a tripped circuit, change a tire, maintain a yard and so much more. I move through the kitchen and into the living room, heading to the basement so I can flip the breaker.

I'm careful as I descend the stairs, not wanting to slip and break my neck or something stupid. God, I won't hear the end of it if Hudson comes home and finds me lying at the base of the stairs with a broken arm or something. I sigh in relief when I reach the landing. I turn toward the right and freeze, a scream lodging in my throat at the sight of two glowing rabbit masks! Last night in the woods they didn't appear this ominous, but the fact that two of them are standing inside *my* house, in the dark, sends a shiver of dread down my spine.

My breathing turns ragged.

I try to calm my racing heart but it won't listen, it keeps beating overtime as I wait for them to say something.

Are they going to kill me?

Fear flows through me, forcing me to remain in place instead of running for my life. "Run, little Bunny," one of them says. I suck in a sharp intake of air.

"Y-you have to go, my brother and his friends—"

"You have thirty seconds. Run to the woods out back. When we catch you, we're going to fucking ruin that pussy." I gasp but I can't move as I'm suddenly turned on while fear still holds me in a chokehold. When the one on the left takes a single step forward, I snap into action and whirl around, taking the stairs two at a time. Safety forgotten as I push my legs harder to get me out of here, I just pray Hudson, Kye and Van don't come home anytime soon.

I make it upstairs and bolt for the back door, throw it open and use my torch to light the way to the woods. My fear is still present, but need is coiling low in my belly. I was unprepared for them to show up to my house that I share with the boys. I'm grateful Hud and the other's weren't home when those two killed the power.

I break through the first line of trees and come to a halt as I dart my gaze from side to side, trying to find a clear path. As much as I want to be caught, my flight or fight instincts won't allow me to be an easy target. When I hear them exit the house behind me I decide to go straight and slink deeper into the woods. The branches scrape against my skin but I don't feel the sting. I'm too drunk on adrenaline to feel anything.

"When we catch you, we're going to rock your fucking world," I hear them call out. I push my legs harder while trying to keep my steps light. I slow my pace and kill the light on my phone, instantly blinded by the sudden darkness. I give myself a moment to adjust to the lighting. The moon is high in the sky but it offers no light thanks to the thick canopy of the trees. I finally get glimpses of light in the gaps of the trees, so I use that to light my path.

My breath hitches when I hear footfalls to my right. I freeze and shrink back against a nearby tree, trying to hide. When a hand wraps around my throat a scream tears out of me, alerting the others to my position. The sight of a glowing rabbit mask has me clamping my mouth closed, my chest rising and falling in quick succession.

"Going somewhere?" he growls. My mouth pops open but no words come out. He releases his hold on me and takes a step back. My knees nearly give out—I'm no fitness guru and all this running has exhausted the fuck out of me. The sound of rustling leaves draws my attention to the right to see two other masks approaching us.

One of them was out here waiting for me, I never had a chance of outsmarting them.

"Would you look at that, our little bunny got snared," one of the guys taunts as they come to stand on either side of the one that captured me.

"What now?" I rasp out, darting my gaze between the three of them.

"Now, you strip for us," the one in the middle orders.

"I-I..." I clamp my mouth closed. I shouldn't be worried about still being on my period since they proved they didn't care last night. I will myself to remain calm and embrace this moment, I may never get another chance to live out my fantasies and like hell will I allow a little blood to ruin this for me. I grip the hem of my T-shirt and yank it over my head. The three of them groan at the sight of my tits as I didn't bother putting a bra on after my shower earlier. I push my shorts down my legs and kick them to the side.

"Fuck."

"Jesus."

"Amen," the three of them say in unison as I stand here in the middle of the woods in nothing but my thong. Their reaction emboldens my confidence. I slide my hands over my tits and cup them, releasing a heady moan. The three of them push their pants down and grip their cocks. They begin to stroke themselves, bringing a smile to my face as I slowly trail my hands down my sides and grip my thong. I spin around and push it down my legs, bending over so they can have a clear view of my pussy.

"Yeah, baby," one of them praises. Before I can think of my next move, I feel one of them push in behind me and grip the globes of my ass in their hands, pulling another moan from me.

"You still bleeding?" he growls from behind me.

"Yes," I reply without hesitation.

He draws his hand back and smacks my ass. I jerk forward in surprise but he holds me in place. "Good girl," he coos as he slides a finger through my folds as the other two come to stand in front of me with their cocks in their hands. My mouth waters at the sight of them. Without being prompted I drop to my knees, then reach out and grip the one on my right in my hand and suck the other into my mouth, moaning at the taste of him. I tense when I feel the string of my tampon being tugged. "Relax, I *need* to taste this cunt, the blood of Christ is the most holy thing. Never deny me my taste of it."

His gravelly demand sends a shiver down my spine. He parts my folds and pushes his tongue inside me, causing me to release the cock in my mouth with a sharp cry of pleasure. I feel so dirty allowing him to eat my pussy while I'm on my period, but the fact he loves it turns me on more. I can feel my arousal gathering at my core. He continues to feast on my dirty little cunt as I alternate between sucking his friends' dicks. I love that they take control and force me to bend to their will. I don't get a chance to think. Their hands tangle in my hair and force my head onto each of their dicks thrusting into my mouth, loving the sound of my gagging around them.

"Yeah, baby, suck me like that," he praises.

The one on the right wraps his hand around mine and squeezes it. "Harder, strangle my cock with your hand," he demands. I groan, loving the fact they love to fuck hard. I can feel my orgasm building. The one eating my pussy wraps his arms around my thighs, almost like he knows when my orgasm slams into me that my legs will give out.

"Hmmmmm," I moan around one's thick girth, trying to alert them that I'm about to come, rather than pulling back so I don't squirt on his face. He presses in harder against me as he sucks my clit into his mouth. I jerk free of the others' hold and scream as I explode, stars dancing in the corners of my eyes as I come harder than ever. Last night was amazing, but tonight, I don't hold back.

"Squirt on his face," Lefty snaps, and like a slave to their master I do as he says. All three of them groan. Righty sings my praise as he grabs my hand and drags me a couple of steps away, making sure to block my view of the other guy as he slips his mask back on. I stand here stunned and shaking as aftershocks tear through me. He lays down on the forest floor with his cock out, reaches into his pocket and produces a tube of lube. I watch with rapt attention as he lathers his cock.

I gasp when one of the others comes up behind me and cups my tits, tweaking my nipples between his fingers. I throw my head back and moan. "I want to watch you sink that ass down on his cock, baby," he purrs.

"Get that ass over here, bunny." I look down through lust filled eyes and smile, then pull free of his friend's hold and straddle his lap reverse cowgirl style. He grips my ass and runs his fingers over my tight hole. I'm still stretched from last night so his fingers slide inside easily. His two friends stand before me, watching. It turns me on seeing them standing there watching us. When he withdraws his fingers I don't wait for his instructions, I reach between us and grip his shaft, lining it up and slowly sink down onto him.

A bead of sweat begins to form on my brow. I can tell from just the feeling of him that he wasn't the one who took my ass last night, this one has a larger girth and it burns as I slowly ease myself onto him.

Look at me now, Mom, bet you wished I was cursing now instead of taking three cocks.

CHAPTER TEN

KYE

Watching her slowly sink down onto Hudson's waiting dick has me gripping my cock in a vice-like hold. The second he is balls deep inside her, she flings her head back and cries out.

"Fuck her," Van growls from beside me. Not needing to be told twice, I stalk forward and relish in the way her eyes widen at the sight of me dropping to my knees before her. My mask offers me enough light to see the blood coating her inner thighs. I smirk at the sight, knowing Van loves tasting her blood. He says it's the blood of Christ and eating that shit is the purest form of light or some shit.

Hudson grips her under her thighs and draws her back against his chest granting me better access. Fuck, her cunt is the prettiest thing I have ever seen. I reach out and finger through her folds and love the way she begins to tremble. She looks so fucking delicate and I love that we are the ones that get to break her apart and put her back together. I line myself up and lock my eyes onto hers as I slowly push inside her. Her mouth parts and a long drawn out moan slips free. Her cheeks turn a shade of red as I continue to ease inside her, loving the way her pussy clamps down on me as if trying to keep me inside her forever.

Unable to go slow any longer, I reach out and grip the back of her neck and slam the remainder of the way inside her. She arches and screams out in pleasure at the feeling of having two of us inside her at once. I spy Van out of the corner of my eye and grin behind my mask, I knew he wouldn't be able to stay on the sidelines.

"Fuck her and make her come," Van growls. I tighten my hold on the back of her neck as I draw almost all of the way out of her before slamming back inside. The sounds she makes are like music to my ears. Hudson and I manage to find a rhythm that is sending her crazy, her cries growing louder and louder until Van shoves his dick in her mouth. His fingers tangle in her hair, holding her in place as he thrusts ruthlessly inside her mouth.

Van may be a priest and lives to serve others, but when he's behind closed doors, he likes control. He craves it. Hudson and I don't mind, it gets us off when he bosses each of us around. Peyton gags around Van's dick but she doesn't try to pull free. When my pace quickens, she begins to shake and smacks me on my chest. I pull out in time for her to squirt all over the front of my hoodie.

"Fuck, switch with me," I snap. Van and I trade places. I peer down at Peyton and wink. When Van moves between her legs, she focuses on him. I'm ready to grip her chin and force her mouth onto my dick until her eyes widen. I follow her line of sight and balk. Van is keeping his word. He kneels between her legs, wrapping rosary beads around his cock. Peyton's mouth pops open as she gasps when he presses forward. She tries to push away from him but Hudson holds her in place.

"Take it like a good girl," Van growls in a tone I've never heard from him before. He can try to deny it as much as he likes, but he likes Peyton as much as Hud and I do. Pey quits struggling and braces for the feeling of him. To my surprise, I'm so focused on her and her reaction to the sensation of being fucked with rosary beads, I forget about everything else until she cries out when he slams inside her. The unhinged sounds coming from her has my cock twitching. "Shove your dick in her mouth and shut her up," Van snarls. I jerk out of my stupor and do exactly as he says. Peyton bats my hand away when I reach for her hair. It's like Van just fucked the devil into her, as she moans around me and bobs her head up and down like a woman possessed.

At the rate she is sucking and lapping at my dick like it's a lollipop, I know I won't last long—the girl is way too fucking good at sucking dick.

"Ah, fuck, I'm gonna come!" Hudson roars from beneath her. Van thrusts harder, forcing her down onto

Hudson, knowing he needs that final push. Hud shouts out his release. The sound of him coming sends me spiraling. Two more pumps and I fist my hand in Peyton's hair, holding her in place as I spill everything I have down her throat, forcing her to swallow every fucking drop of me.

"Yes, I can feel your cunt wanting to come. Don't you dare come until I do." She whimpers around me at Van's order. I slowly ease out of her and stroke her cheek.

"I need to come," she pleads as she reaches out and grips the front of Van's hoodie, holding on for dear life. Hudson has no choice but to remain where he is as Van slams inside her with a punishing intensity, but she weathers it. The cries of ecstasy tumbling from her lips tells us she is loving everything he is inflicting on her.

"Come!" Van roars. Both of them join each other in euphoric bliss a second later. Van rips free of her and lifts his mask enough to expose his mouth. She squirts and he catches it in his mouth, swallowing everything she offers him.

He is one kinky fucker.

She has no time to come down before Van is pushing two fingers inside her dripping cunt. Her cries die out when he pulls free and uses her blood to paint a cross on her forehead. I bite back my laugh, he did the same thing to her last night.

"You've been blessed with the best," Hudson says with humor clear in his tone. Van growls but says nothing as he climbs to his feet and fixes his clothes. I do the same, then help Peyton to her feet. Her legs are shaking so badly she can't support her own weight. Hudson gathers her clothes but I don't miss the sight of him pocketing her thong. I hold her waist as he helps her into her shorts then pulls her shirt over her head. The second he steps back she flops forward, burying her face in my chest.

"Just leave me here," she mumbles, making the three of us chuckle. I bend and scoop her up into my arms and begin walking back toward the house. "What are you doing?" she asks in a panic.

"Taking you home," Hudson answers.

She tries to fight against my hold. "No, my step brother and his friends will be there."

"They aren't home," Van says.

"How do you know that?" she fires back.

The three of us remain silent for a second, trying to think of a good lie. "I saw them at the church, the priest was in a confession with Annika," Hudson lies with ease. I spy Van cringing out of the corner of my eye.

"Oh," is all she says. I know she is thinking the worst of Van right now and it's clear as day on her face that she is jealous. None of us speak again until we reach the edge of the woods and can see the house in the distance. I slowly lower her to her feet and don't step back until I'm sure she's steady. When she looks at each of us, I begin to worry she can see our faces beneath the masks. She begins to nibble her bottom lip and twists the hem of her shirt in her hands, clearly nervous. "Will I see you guys again?" she asks barely above a whisper.

"Yes," the three of us answer without hesitation, causing her eyes to widen.

"When?" she presses as she looks at each of us.

"Next weekend," I respond immediately.

"Okay," she says with a sexy smirk. She takes one last lingering look at each of us before she sighs and trudges back to the house, while the three of us just stand here waiting for her to disappear inside.

"We're fucked," Hud mutters.

"So fucked," I concur.

"I need to quit my job," Van adds. Both of us snap our heads toward him.

"What?' Hudson rasps.

Van shrugs and pushes his hands into his pockets. "I can't be a priest and lust after a girl who is into some of the darkest shit, like me. I've never felt so alive. Last night she breathed life back into me and tonight... Fuck, she is perfect."

"She was made for us," Hudson growls.

"I'm keeping her," I declare.

"*We're* keeping her," Van corrects.

"We're so fucked, she will figure out it's the three of us," Hud mutters.

"Then we make the choice easy. We get her to fall for us without the masks on, so when the time comes, it will be too late for her, she won't have to choose."

"How the fuck do we do that, Kye?" Van bites.

"We each get burner phones and start texting her. We make a group chat and force the little minx to open up about her feelings about her roommates." Both the guys laugh and agree to my plan.

Time to play on the dark side, bunny.

CHAPTER ELEVEN
PEYTON

I can still feel the ghost of them inside me.

Every step I take I feel them. I didn't see any of the guys when they came home last night. After I showered, I passed out and didn't wake until Hudson started banging on my door this morning, demanding I get up and get ready for church. The drive was short and filled with silence but it wasn't awkward. I was surprised when Hudson announced Kye would be joining us.

Sitting here in the back row with Tess feels wrong. I feel like God is judging me right now. I can't shake the feeling that I am being watched and it's eerie. I know I shouldn't be here, I sinned so badly but fuck, I can't find it within myself to care. If those three masked guys showed up right now, I would run out of this church with them and let them fuck me in broad daylight against the side of the church.

You only live once, so I may as well enjoy it and deal with burning for the rest of eternity in hell later.

"Did we raise enough to fix your house?" Tess whispers, pulling me from my thoughts.

"I didn't ask," I admit, feeling like an asshole. I should have asked Van or Mom yesterday but I just... I couldn't focus on anything aside from meeting my guys.

Wait!

My guys?

We fucked twice and now I am labeling them as mine? I need to get my head checked, pronto!

"I heard from my mom and a couple of the other ladies that they put in extra cash because they heard you were living with Van and wanted you away from their priest before you could corrupt him." I snort loudly and quickly cover my mouth, then slouch down in my seat when everyone swings their head toward me.

"Carry on, Father," I mutter, earning a glare from Van at the front of the church. If I didn't have the entire town's attention on me right now, I'd flip the asshole off but I manage to refrain. Tess shakes with silent laughter. I give her the stink eye and pull out my phone, frowning when I see a text from an unknown number.

Unknown - Did you have fun last night

Me - Who the hell is this?

. . .

*Unknown added, Goliath and Saint to the chat

Me - Who the fuck are you and who are those other two you added?

I sit here bouncing my leg up and down, my chest is tight with hope. I want it to be my masked men but I don't want to build myself up in case it isn't them. The disappointment would be a killer.

Goliath - Oh, Bunny, did you forget us already?

I gasp and quickly cover my mouth. Tess shoots me a look but I wave her off and quickly type out a reply.

Me - How could I forget you when I can still feel the ghost of you inside me.

Unknown - This is gonna be the longest week of my life.

Goliath changes Unknowns name to Mac

. . .

Me - I'm assuming these aren't your real names?

Mac - What gave it away.

Me - The fact none of you will show me your faces but are fine to fuck me.

Goliath - If only you knew who we really were… I think she might be trying to figure out who we are @Mac

Me - What the hell does Mac stand for?

Goliath - Mac Daddy

I bite down on my lip to keep from laughing out loud.

Goliath - I don't know if I can wait a week to be inside you again.

Mac - My cock is hard just thinking about how good you sucked it.

Me - Now I'm clenching my thighs together in fucking church!

Mac - Want to be a sinner?

Me - 😿

Me - I sinned last night and the night before and during the week with my priest.

Mac - You fucked your priest?

Me - No!

Goliath - But you want to?

Me - What is this? Twenty questions?

Mac - Send me a picture of our pussy and I'll stop harassing you.

Goliath - What he said 🔺

Me - I'm in church!

Mac - So?

Goliath - Your point?

I debate how to do it. Tess seems distracted and I did wear a dress today... Fuck it. I shift subtly and make sure no one is watching when I slip my phone under my dress and snap a pic of my lace covered pussy and push send. It takes a minute for their responses to come in.

Goliath - Fuck, baby!

Mac - I'm so hard.

Goliath - I need to see it, baby. Move that lace to the side and show me how wet you are for us.

Mac - My mouth is watering for a taste of that cunt.

Need pulses inside me, I've never felt so aroused until meeting these three. They know I love the chase, and that the masks add to their allure. Some may view this as sick and depraved but haven't you ever wished for a man to chase you around, give you everything you have been too ashamed to ask for out loud? That the fact you have no idea who they are only makes it easier to demand what you want? No judgment, just pure carnal need to be fucked. I dart my gaze around and see everyone is focused on Van, who stands behind his podium giving his boring ass service. I check to make sure Tess is still not paying me any attention, then discreetly shift my panties to the side and widen my legs. My period stopped this morning which I'm grateful for because I don't think I would have sent this picture otherwise. I can feel how wet I am already and know they will love the sight of my dripping cunt, knowing they are the reason.

I check the picture and cringe, I shouldn't be sending

this but I want to live in this fantasy for as long as I can. This is the type of shit I have craved. I love feeling dirty and this whole thing feels wrong and taboo and that just adds to the appeal. I suck in a deep breath and push send.

Since I'm going to hell anyway, I may as well enjoy my moments on earth.

CHAPTER TWELVE

VAN

"John 3:16 once said…" When the phone Kye gave me pings again with another message, I ignore it and flip the page in my Bible but I accidentally knock the phone and unlock it. The second the pictures appear on my screen, my eyes widen and my train of thought evaporates as I stare down at Peyton's drenched pussy.

Goliath - Fuck, baby, let me fuck you tonight.

Mac - I need to sink my cock inside that tight pussy.

I snap my head up and spot her instantly in the back with Tess, biting down on her lips with a smile on her face as she types on her phone. My mouth goes dry. I reach up and stroke the collar I wear around my neck. I shouldn't be thinking about fucking her while I stand here, but all I can think about is how incredible her pussy felt wrapped around my cock last night and how delicious her cum tasted.

"Father Pierce?" I shake my head and dart my gaze to Tabitha who stares up at me from the front row with a concerned look on her face. I flick my gaze back to Peyton who is now looking directly at me, I tear my gaze from hers and plaster a smile on my face.

"Forgive me, I was lost in thought. Please give me one moment," I say, then pretend to find the correct page in the Bible but type out a reply to the group chat.

Saint - When everyone leaves the church you stay behind and head to confession, you will be punished for disrespecting the Lord's house. Before you even think about searching for us just know you will never figure it out. Make me wait and you will be going longer than a week without a release.

I lock the phone and ignore its constant vibration as I return to my service. Peyton will pay for this. I'm now forced to deliver this fucking service with a raging hard-on! I still have to speak to her mother and stepfather after this. I force all thoughts about how amazing their daughter tastes from my mind and focus on the here and now or else I'll drag Peyton into the confession chamber now and fuck her brains out just to teach her a lesson for daring to send a picture when I wasn't prepared. I cut a glance to Hudson and Kye who sit in the middle row on the opposite side, both of them sitting there with broad smiles on their faces.

They knew what they were doing when they asked for that picture, they wanted me to lose control. Those fuckers will pay for this stunt. If they think they will be joining us in the confession chamber, they are dead fucking wrong. This is a punishment for them as much as it is for her.

"Thank you so much, Father Pierce." I smile at Lenior and place my hand on top of hers as she holds my other.

"It wasn't me, the community came together and as a whole we made this happen. I'm grateful we are able to help both you and Ken get your home fixed," I say.

"Yeah, as soon as we get the plumbing fixed, I can start on the repairs," Hudson adds, earning an eye roll from Peyton who stands behind her parents fidgeting.

"Regardless, we are thankful that you could pull this all together in such a short time, Father." I wave away Ken's thanks.

"We were blessed." Both of them smile and bid me goodbye. Hudson wraps an arm around Peyton's shoulders and drags her into his side. She shoves him away from her and smacks him on the chest just as Kye appears behind her.

"Want to go to the lake?" Kye asks. Peyton's face falls and we all wait to hear her answer.

"Uh, I made plans but you guys should go and I can meet you there after I finish this thing I have to do." Kye coughs to mask his laughter. Hudson on the other hand just stands there and laughs.

"Yeah, right on, little sis." She scowls at her brother and places her hands on her hips.

"Do you have to be so..."

"Handsome?" he answers for her. She growls and stomps her foot, which has my brows hitting my hairline.

"Annoying," she grits out. "Now, if you'll all excuse me, I need a moment alone with my... ah, prayers and I like to um, pray in private." She fumbles over her words and anyone with good sense can tell she is full of shit, but none of us call her on it. Kye and Hudson say their goodbyes to Peyton, then look at me expectantly.

"I have paperwork to catch up on. I'll meet you guys there in an hour." Hudson rolls his lips over his teeth and nods. Kye just smirks and wags his brows, I know for a fact these two idiots aren't going to leave. I'd bet good money that they will hide out and then sneak into the other confessional and fuck while getting off to the sounds she'll make. I leave her to fake pray while I head into my office to change. I refuse to look at anything in my office, not wanting to feel judged.

Peyton has made me lose control and she needs to be punished for doing it. I nearly lost my cool today in front of the whole town. Once I'm changed, I grab my mask and slip out of my office. I make sure the back entrance of the church is locked, I know the guys would have locked the front for me. I secure my mask and stalk to the front. I smirk when I see she isn't where I left her, which means she is being a good girl and waiting for me. I scan the church to make sure it's empty, the last thing I need is for someone to be lurking in here and find their priest fucking his girl in the confessional.

Fuck!

I pause and sift through my thoughts, is that what she has become? Is she ours?

Yes.

I don't allow myself to dwell on that, Peyton may not know it yet, but the three of us have claimed her as ours and whether she likes it or not, we're going to keep her. I approach the wooden structure and take a deep breath. What I'm about to do is going to cross a line I can never come back from. I want to feel guilty for committing so many sins with her but I can't. I regret nothing when it concerns her. From the moment she moved in next door, I knew she would stir shit up around here, I just didn't realize that she was made for me—*for us.*

"Face the wall," I growl. I hear her shuffle around, obeying my demand. When silence falls, I pull the door open and step inside the cramped space. I latch the door behind me and love how tight the space is, we're already touching without meaning to. Her shoulders rise and fall, her back plastered to my front. I reach out and wrap her hair around my fist, forcing her head back. She gasps when she meets my gaze, the glow of my mask illuminating the tiny space.

"Who are you?" she breathes out.

"Your sins made of flesh," I grit out. Her mouth parts but no words follow. I use my grip on her hair to force her forward. She braces her hands on the small bench type seat. I run my hand down her back, loving the shiver that rolls through her. I grip the hem of her dress and bunch it around her waist, then run my hands over the globes of her ass. A wanton moan escapes her when I draw my hand back and smack her ass, relishing the sight of her ass turning red.

"Fuck me, please," she begs. I wrap my index finger around the thin string that runs through her cheeks, slowly pull it free of its hiding spot and push it to the side.

"This is about me. You don't get to come. Am I clear?" She whimpers but doesn't respond, forcing me to tug on her hair until she yelps. "Am. I. Clear?"

She darts her tongue out to moisten her lips. "I want to say yes but you all fuck me so good I don't know if I'll be able to stop it." Her defiance should piss me off but it has the opposite effect, knowing she can't help but fall victim to our savagery has the darkness inside me spreading like a virus, begging me to claim this perfect girl.

I release her and free my cock. I grip my shaft and run it through her slick folds, groaning at how fucking wet she is. "Beg me."

"Please, I want you to fuck me," she answers without hesitation. I press inside her, loving how her body accepts me without restriction—I'm not even fully sheathed inside her and she's trembling. A gasp escapes her when the divider is opened. She snaps her head to the side to see Hudson and Kye both at the divider, wearing their masks and watching her.

"He's going to fuck you while *I* fuck him," Kye growls. I bite back my smirk, I knew those two wouldn't be able to stay away. Her pussy flutters around my cock, knowing they are about to fuck turns this dirty little girl on. I draw back as far as I can, then thrust forward. She cries out and Hudson and Kye both grunt next door.

"Holy fuck, this is too much." She pants as I continue to fuck her, my grip on her waist is bruising.

"You like knowing they are fucking?" I grunt as I slam inside her again.

"Yes. I fucking love it. I want to watch them," she answers. I swivel us around so I'm sitting on the bench.

"Bounce on my cock while you watch them." She braces her hands on the wall, then turns her head so she can watch them through the divider then starts bouncing on my dick reverse cowgirl. I reach around and cup her tits through her dress, loving the sound of the strangled moan she releases.

"You like this, Bunny?" Kye growls.

"Yes," she pants out.

"Fuck, his cock feels so good in my ass, baby," Hudson groans.

"Oh shit, I need to come," she cries. I push my mask up, exposing my mouth, and order her to come as I sink my teeth into her shoulder. She screams so loud God himself would have heard. My grip on her waist turns fucking brutal as I force her up and down on my cock, chasing my own release. Kye and Hudson finish a second before I blow. Shudders roll through me as I try to catch my breath. Fuck, her pussy is clenching my dick so perfectly, milking me of every damn drop.

"You walk out of here and don't look back, Bunny. We'll see you next week," Hudson pants out. I feel her deflate at his dismissal but she needs to leave before us. She sucks in a deep breath and slowly moves. The second I slip free of her, I feel cold without the heat of her wrapped around me.

I'll lose the collar for her and continue to sin. I have no doubt in my mind that Peyton Jordan will be ours.

When I pull up to the lake, I spot Van and Hudson's cars. I park, climb out and smile at the sight of the three of them wrestling in the water. After I left the church, I rushed home to shower and change, there was no way I could come here without cleaning the cum out of me. Fuck, just the thought of what happened has me clenching my thighs. He was rough and used me to get off. He didn't ask permission, he just took. Add the two next door fucking and I was a puddle of need. Ever since I saw Kye and Hudson fucking, I have wanted to see it again and being allowed to openly watch today was an experience I will never forget.

"Peyton!" I shake my head, chasing those thoughts away as I look at the guys. Kye is running toward me with a broad grin on his face. I sigh knowing what's coming. I raise my arms, which just has him laughing as he scoops me off the ground. I wrap my arms and legs around him as he grips the globes of my ass, sending a shiver through me at the memory of my ass being spanked earlier. I smile down at Kye. "Took you long enough to get here."

I roll my eyes. "I had to go home and get my bathing suit," I answer as he reaches the water's edge. I tighten my hold on him as he walks us toward the others, then gasp and press against him even tighter as the cold water laps at my skin.

"Keep pushing those tits in my face, baby and I may just take a bite." I stare at Kye and shake my head.

"You wouldn't dare." A dark glint enters his eyes and I know without a doubt, Kye would keep true to his word.

"Little sis, where's my love at?" I turn to Hudson and quirk a brow.

"You want me wrapped around you like a monkey?" I tease.

A devious smirk graces Hudson's gorgeous face. "Nah, babe, I want you wrapped around me like a condom."

"Eww, why?" I screech.

"Because then I would be inside you." My jaw drops. Before I can gather my thoughts, Kye passes me off to Hudson. I instinctively wrap my arms and legs around him. Suddenly the chill of the water can't be felt, the humor in Hudson's eyes vanishes as he stares up at me with a look I have never seen before, *hunger*. I suck in a sharp breath when I feel someone press against my back. I peer over my shoulder and lock eyes with Van's stunning baby blues. When he grips my waist, I tense. Van leans in and ghosts his lips over the shell of my ear.

"In case you haven't noticed, you have all our attention and each of us would gladly sin just so we could be inside you." An inferno erupts through my veins, my body temperature skyrockets, and my breaths come in short rapid pants. I whip my head to the other side when I feel Kye brush against my arm. The ravenous desire I see in his brown eyes has my heart skipping a beat.

"We're here!" The four of us all jerk apart at the sound of Tess's voice. My friend stands on the bank with pursed lips as she looks between all of us.

"Saved by Tess," Kye grunts.

"Pity, we had plans for you," Hudson says low enough for only us to hear as Tess and a few others she invited trudge into the water. When I feel Van press against my back, I have to swallow my groan.

"Next time, don't invite your friend," he growls.

I keep my gaze ahead as I answer. "I thought you said I wouldn't want to meet the person without the collar?"

A dark chuckle escapes him. "I removed the collar the moment you moved into town." My eyes widen and my breath hitches as he skims his fingers down my side and places an open mouth kiss on the spot my masked man bit me. "Next time, don't hide the mark with makeup." He releases me and moves to join Hudson and Kye who are talking to some other guys. Tess comes to me, darting her gaze from me to the guys.

"What was that?" she asks.

"He knew about the mark," I mutter.

Tess's face contorts. "What mark?" I shake my head and clamp my mouth closed.

How the fuck did Van know about my mark?

I look down at my shoulder and note the bruise is still hidden by my concealer. "Pey, are you okay?" I plaster a fake smile on my face and nod.

"Yeah, just a lot on my mind," I lie.

"Girl, the sexual tension between the four of you is fucking strong. You need to get laid or let one of them slip inside you just to take the edge off." I choke on my own spit.

"Tess!" I hiss, drawing the attention of those around us. When I invited Tess to join us at the lake, I didn't think she would invite others but it appears I was wrong. At least twenty others have joined us and I can't help but feel annoyed at myself.

If I didn't invite her, what would have happened between me and the guys?

We're still out at the lake long after the sun has set and darkness blankets the sky. Hudson and some of the other guys made a bonfire. Most of the girls who came are weary of me. Tess assures me it's just because they are worried

I'm going to steal all the available guys in town, which had me snorting. What I can't piece together is why the girls constantly shoot weird looks at Kye and Hudson. They have all tried to speak to Van but none have spoken to the other two.

"Here." I turn away from the crowd gathered around the bonfire to see Kye standing beside me with a hoodie in his hand. I smile my thanks and slip it on. My smile widens when the scent of him engulfs me and I find myself relaxing.

"Thanks," I mutter.

"Why are you standing back here?" he questions.

I shrug. "I don't know, I guess I'm just not in a talking mood."

"Liar."

I narrow my eyes at him playfully. "Fine. I'll answer your question if you tell me why none of those girls will speak to you or Hud?"

He laughs. The sound reverberates through me and I can't help but beam up at him. He throws his arm around my shoulders and draws me into his side. At that moment both Van and Hudson look over at us. I expect them to look angry or something but the sight of them smiling just floors me.

"That's easy to answer. Ever since Hud and I got caught making out, the whole town has treated us like we are some infectious disease." I gasp and swivel out of his hold, then balk up at him.

"What?" I screech. I can feel the others' eyes on me but I ignore them.

Kye stuffs his hands in his pockets and shrugs his shoulders like it's not a big deal. "It is what it is, babe. I don't care what any of these pricks think. I like fucking Hud and neither of us have an issue with it."

"So are you two like... *together?*"

He smiles and shakes his head. "No. We enjoy it but we aren't committed to each other in that way." A surge of hope flares inside me but I snuff that bitch out. I'm already fucking three guys and there is no way I could handle another three. I really like Hudson, Van and Kye, but to cross a line with them would be stupid. My masked guys give me everything I need sexually but is that all it would be? No emotional attachment, just sex? "Ask me what you want to know, Pey, I can see a question swirling in your eyes."

I dart my tongue out to moisten my lips, not missing how he tracks the movement. "Why do you both stay in this town then? I wouldn't be able to handle the judgment daily," I admit.

He sighs and nods. "I hate living here and so does Hud but we stay because of Van."

My brows crash together. "Why?"

"Because someone like me doesn't get accepted often." I whirl around and come face to face with Van. He presses in until his chest is pressed against mine. "I have..." He purses his lips trying to find the right words. "Certain tastes and I hate being judged for it. I found my faith and shut the door on that part of me, knowing I would never find someone to share those urges with until recently." I swallow, my mouth is suddenly dry.

"What type of tastes?" I blurt without thinking.

I jump when I feel Kye's lips brush against the shell of my ear. "The type you love."

My balls are so heavy it's starting to get hard to walk!

All of us have been on edge all week, counting down the days until we can have her again. So many times this week I have nearly fucked up and told her the truth. Peyton has been spending more time around us and I can tell she likes us, but thinks it wrong for her to want all three of us. It's Thursday night and we're all sitting in the living room watching a movie. Van is in the love seat while Pey is lying with her feet on Kye's lap and her head in mine. I may be horny as fuck, but being able to have her so relaxed and allowing us to touch her freely this past week has been incredible.

Her phone rings with an incoming FaceTime call, breaking me from my thoughts. When she lifts it and sees it's her father a broad smile stretches across her beautiful face. I expect her to sit up and walk out of the room so her dad doesn't see her with her head in my lap but she surprises me when she answers it.

"Hey, Daddy."

His face fills the screen and he beams at his daughter. "Hey, baby girl, how are you?"

"I'm good. How are you? Where are you?"

"I'm great actually." There's a hint of excitement to his tone which has her studying him.

"What happened?" she presses. The three of us are so invested in this conversation, Van turns the volume on the TV down so we can listen in better.

"I spoke to your mom, she told me about what happened to her house."

"Oh, sorry. I forgot to mention that. The town raised enough to help her and Ken with the plumbing. Hudson and Kye are going to help them rebuild the downstairs." I flick my gaze to Kye who has the same dumbfounded look on his face, she talks about us like she has told her father about us and that shit has me wanting to beat my fists against my chest.

"That's great. But, she did tell me something you forgot to mention." Peyton begins gnawing on her bottom lip nervously. "You got some explaining to do, young lady." I look at my boys and find they are all staring at her with rapt attention.

Peyton sighs. "I was going to tell you but then... everything just changed and I've been busy and it just slipped my mind." She's lying and now I need to know what the fuck she is hiding.

"P, this is something we should have discussed first." He sounds hurt that she didn't tell him about whatever this is.

"I know, Daddy," she whispers. "I just... I didn't know how to tell you. You know what Moms like and she would have cried or made a big deal about it, and I just didn't want to deal with it."

Brice sighs and scrubs a hand down his face. I've never formally met her father but I've heard a lot about him from her mom, and he seems like a good guy. "I get it, baby girl, I just wish you would have told me. Your mother is freaking out."

Peyton rolls her lips over teeth to keep from smiling. "Lucky I'm not living with her right now then, huh?" Brice shakes his head and laughs.

"Jesus, P. A father doesn't appreciate getting a message from his teenage daughter telling him she is living with three guys. You sure know how to get my blood pressure up."

Peyton bursts out laughing and I love the fucking sound, it's so beautiful that it brings a smile to my face. "Hey, one of them is a priest," she fires back, then shoots Van a wink. The fucker just rolls his eyes but even he can't help but smile at her.

"They're the worst!" Brice claps back, causing Peyton

to laugh. Van snorts and starts mumbling something under his breath. "Are you being *safe*?"

Peyton turns a bright shade of red. "Dad!" she scolds.

Brice raises his hand in surrender, the three of us all laughing at her expense. "Oh, so I assume they can hear?" he presses. Peyton groans and nods. "Well, good. Safety is paramount, boys—"

"Dad, oh my God," Peyton snaps, then rushes out of the room with our laughter following her.

"I like him," Kye announces and wags his brows.

I shove the fucker. "He wouldn't think much of us if he knew," I say.

"He said *boys*, he never stipulated just *one*," Van mumbles. I think back to a second ago and realize he's right. Her father warned all of us—does he know? I shake that thought away, of course he doesn't know because not even she does.

"What is she hiding?" I wonder aloud.

"No fucking clue but I plan to find out," Van growls.

"Our girl is hiding shit and I don't fucking like it," Kye grits out.

"We will make her tell us tomorrow," I declare. Our conversation is cut off when she saunters back into the room and reclaims her position from earlier like nothing happened. It's taking everything inside me not to press her for details right now. I run my fingers through her hair, loving the soft mewl that escapes her. The three of us have never been so content before. We're all sitting here, watching some stupid sci-fi movie she picked because Theo James is in it and apparently *Divergent* is the best movie, because he claims his girl and stops at nothing to save her.

Each of us have acted like we were interested in it when she told us but the truth is, we would have sat for hours watching a blank screen if she told us to. All any of us want is just to be around her. Wearing the masks is becoming harder. I want her to know it's us and to want us in the same fucking way we crave her.

Saint - You have twenty minutes to be in the woods behind the church.

The three of us took off after dinner earlier, telling her we had some shit to do. She looked torn and like she wanted to protest but I know she's been looking forward to this weekend as much as we have. I can tell the guys want to confess it's us behind the masks as well, but each of us are worried she'll run and never speak to any of us again. Fuck, the thought of her denying us has my chest aching.

Bunny - OMW

. . .

I smirk at her instant reply, I have no doubt that she has been waiting for that message all damn night since we left.

"Fuck, man, it's a long weekend so does that mean we get her for the whole thing?" Kye asks. It's Easter weekend and most of the town has shut down for the four days. Unlike us, Van had to work today and will work Easter Sunday.

"Yeah," Van answers. I look down at the basket of chocolates we got her and an idea slams into me. I reach down and retrieve the chocolate Easter Bunny and twirl it in my hands.

"Asshole, don't eat that!" Kye snaps.

"Oh, I plan to use this bad boy to get our girl off then eat and lick the melted chocolate out of her pussy before we fuck her." Both of them stare at me with blank expressions for a second before they are both darting for the basket. I laugh at the idiots, tonight is going to be fucking epic and I plan to take my time with her. If this is going to be our last weekend with her, then I am going to make the fucking most of it because I need her to want us. I can't go back to not having her in our lives. She is perfect and fits the three of us.

Our laughter dies off when we hear leaves rustling. We all share a look before we secure our masks in place and take off into the woods, ready to chase our girl and make her submit... make her want and need us until she can't live without us. This weekend, we are going to make her see there is no her without the three of us. Peyton Jordan has turned our fucking lives upside down and we aren't mad about it. We all know she will be weary of the stigma that will follow us, when people learn she is not only fucking her stepbrother but her priest and their best friend.

CHAPTER FIFTEEN
PEYTON

I suck in a deep breath and square my shoulders as I walk through the woods. I don't bother with a flashlight, I know they will find me with ease. I keep my head on a swivel and trudge ahead. I keep walking for a few minutes before feeling the hairs on the back of my neck stand up. My breathing amps up.

They're watching me!

I can feel their eyes on me. My skin prickles with awareness and I know it's only a matter of time before the chase is on, so I keep calm and act like I don't know they are near. I continue forward toward a large tree, the second I round the trunk I break out into a sprint and head deeper into the woods. The sound of their footfalls pounding the dirt behind me has me pushing myself harder to escape them. As much as I want to be caught, I refuse to make this easy on them.

"You're only making this harder on yourself, Bunny!" one of them shouts from behind me, something in his voice seems familiar but I brush it off as I break through some thick shrubs and gasp when I spot a creek up ahead. It isn't the creek that has my heart pounding inside my chest, it's the sight of one of my masked men, standing at the edge with his mask glowing bright in the moonlight.

A scream lodges in my throat when a body presses against my back and a hand wraps around my throat from behind. The plastic of his mask rubs against my tender flesh as he speaks low.

"On your knees." He releases me so I can obey his demand. I sink to the rough ground. I was smart enough to wear sneakers and jeans this time, knowing I would be forced to run and I didn't want my knees getting busted up and having the guys asking me questions about it tomorrow. "Get my cock out." I reach up and begin undoing his pants as the other two draw in closer. When his cock springs free, my mouth waters at the sight of it. I don't need any prompting, I wrap my hand around his shaft and pump. His head rolls back as a groan escapes him. I dart my tongue out and lick him from base to tip, loving the feel of his silky skin. I flick my eyes to meet his as I suck his cock into my mouth.

A whimper escapes me when fingers tangle in my hair and force me to take him deeper. My hands wrap around his thighs as I relax my throat, trying to take him deeper but my gag reflex is an asshole and I begin choking on him.

The dark chuckles that sound out around us doesn't deter me, I know how much they love to hear me. I dart my gaze side to side to see the other two standing there with their dicks in their hands. I reach out and grip each of them, making sure to keep my grip tight and firm, just how they like it.

I alternate between sucking each of them, relishing at the sounds each of them make each time my lips wrap around their cocks.

"Stop!" the one on the right growls. I release them and pull back, gasping for air. I swipe the spit from my chin. "On your feet and strip." I do as he says and stand. I hate that I'm always the one who is naked but never them, the only thing I get to see is their cocks. It's not enough they hide their faces from me but they also shield their bodies. My shirt is the first to go, I made sure to wear my black lace set tonight. I kick my sneakers off, then pop the button on my jeans and slowly push them down my legs, loving the feel of their eyes on me the entire time. When I stand before them in nothing but my bra and panties, I suddenly feel unsure.

I haven't felt like this since the first time, but now suddenly I feel uncertain because in the past week, it isn't just them who haunt my thoughts. I can't seem to stop thinking about Van, Hudson and Kye. Those three have somehow wormed themselves inside me and I'm starting to realize I have feelings for them, *big* feelings.

"On your back," the one in the middle snaps, drawing

me from my thoughts. I do as he demands and force myself to focus on the moment and not dwell on my thoughts. It doesn't matter what I feel for the other three, I can never have them. "Legs open." I bend at the knees and open them as wide as I can, they may not be able to see it because of the poor lighting but I can feel I have already soaked through my panties. The one in the middle drops to his knees before me and reaches inside the pocket of his hoodie and pulls out a... is that a chocolate bunny?

"When you leave tonight, you'll find a gift basket at the back of the church. We borrowed a few gifts, hope you don't mind?" the one on the left says. My attention is brought back to the guy between my legs when he pushes my panties to the side and unwraps the bunny. My eyes widen when he runs the tip of the bunny ears through my slick folds. I arch off the hard ground.

The one on the right shifts and pushes me up so he can sit behind me, I rest back against his chest as I watch with rapt attention as the bunny continues to circle my clit, drawing a long moan from me. The one behind reaches around and yanks the cups of my bra down and frees my tits—they feel so heavy and are begging to be played with. I cry out when he pinches my nipples between his fingers, a scream ripping out of me a second later when the other pushes the fucking rabbit inside me.

"Fuck!" I hiss.

"Take it," the one behind me growls as the other guy

continues to use the bunny to fuck me. The last guy comes to stand beside us and rubs his pre-cum across my lips.

"Suck it." I do as I'm commanded and suck him into my mouth. The pressure inside me begins to build but the feeling slowly ebbs away as the damn chocolate starts melting inside me. The moment he yanks it free of my pussy, I whimper around the other's cock. "Don't worry, Bunny, he's gonna eat that cunt clean and make you squirt on his face."

True to his word, his friend does exactly that, he pushes his hot wet tongue inside my tight little hole. The one behind begins rubbing something on my nipples. I look down to see him using Easter eggs. Oh fuck, they are covering me in chocolate. I gasp and release his cock with a wet pop when the guy between my legs starts rubbing the melted bunny on my ass.

"Don't worry," the one behind me purrs. "We'll lick you clean before we're finished with you." His words have heat coiling low in my belly. I can feel my orgasm cresting, sounds tumbling from my lips that would have my mother blushing. The sensations they are dragging out of me are sinister. I'm nothing but an instrument in their hands, they can play me better than I could ever play myself.

"Come on his face, Bunny," the one on my side growls as he fists himself. His words are my undoing.

My back arches and my scream pierces the air "Fuck!" Before I can control it, I squirt all over him. He opens his mouth and holds my cum in his mouth as the other guy steps forward, lifts his mask and presses his lips to the others'. My eyes widen when I realize they are both drinking my fucking cum!

"Do you like watching them taste you?" the person behind me asks as the other two break their kiss, then slip their masks back into place and look at me.

"Yes," I answer truthfully.

"Good because we have a surprise for you tonight, Bunny. Turn around and sit on my cock." I do as he says and straddle his lap, line him up with my entrance and slowly sink down onto his cock, relishing the burn of him stretching me. "Fuck, I missed this cunt," he forces out when he bottoms out inside me. A hand lands on the center of my back, forcing me to lay flat against his chest. I shiver when I feel the coolness of the lube being massaged into my tight asshole. I've become a whore for anal—I never thought I would enjoy it, but now I fucking crave it. The feeling of having two cocks inside me at once is addictive and makes me feel so full.

This time when he slides inside my ass I don't tense, there is hardly much resistance because I'm so turned on. He tries to go slow but I'm greedy for them. I press back and force him the remainder of the way inside me. We cry out at the feeling. "Fuck, Bunny," he croaks.

"You feel so good inside me," I purr as I grind against them.

"You ready for your surprise?" the one beneath me

asks. I frown and nod. The guy behind me groans, I peer over my shoulder and my jaw drops.

"Oh, fuck, that is hot," I mutter as I take in the sight of the last guy sinking his cock into the other—this is something out of one of my wildest fantasies. I never in a million fucking years ever thought I would get to live this out. I have two cocks inside me while one of the guys is being fucked behind me by his friend.

My cock twitches inside Hudson and he groans, which just causes Peyton to whimper. The sight of me fucking him while he is inside her is euphoric for all of us. I never thought a moment like this would happen, but when Van told us how much she loved watching me fuck Hudson beside them in the confessional, I just knew we had to try it and I'm so fucking glad we did. Peyton gasps when Van wraps his rosary beads around her neck and tightens his hold, restricting her airway.

He's such a kinky fucker.

"Asphyxiation will heighten your pleasure, Bunny." She nods shakily. I draw back and slam inside Hudson, forcing him forward, the four of us all moan at the feeling. I'm the one who sets the pace tonight and I refuse to bust a nut early, I want to draw this moment out for as long as I can. Van meets me thrust for thrust.

"Oh fuck, yes, please don't stop," Peyton cries out. I reach around and grip Hudson's throat, knowing he loves it when I choke the fuck out of him. He groans in pleasure and pushes back against me harder. I hiss and tighten my grip on his throat.

"Fuck me, Mac," he growls, using the stupid name he gave me in the chat. Peyton snaps her head to the side and watches us with a hunger in her blue eyes. She loves being fucked by the three of us but she loves this as well.

"Fuck him harder," she growls, all our movements turning jerky at her demand. I look down at Van to find his focus is on her.

"Do it," V growls. I release my hold on Hudson only to freeze when Peyton lifts one of her hands from Van's chest and wraps it around Hudson's throat. She stares directly into his eyes and my breath hitches when her eyes widen.

Can she tell it's him?

Van chooses that moment to grip her waist and forces her to move. She blinks rapidly for a second before she follows his lead and moves in sync with me without even realizing it. I can feel my balls tightening with the need to come, but I fight against the urge. Tonight I need the four of us to come as one.

"Tighter," Hudson grits out. Peyton obeys and strengthens her hold on his neck. Van pinches her nipples between his fingers. Peyton throws her head back and screams.

"Oh shit, yes just like that, please," she begs.

"Fuck, yes, make me come," Hudson growls.

"Get there, Saint," I force out through clenched teeth.

"I'm with you," Van snaps. My pace turns punishing as I thrust in and out of Hudson at a ruthless pace.

"Oh God, yes, fuck, I'm gonna come," she shouts.

"Fuck!" Hudson roars as he comes. Peyton follows him over the edge screaming. Van tumbles behind them and I'm the last to fall. I come harder than I ever have, shudders rolling through me without restraint, as I empty everything I have inside Hud. All of us are panting and gasping for air. This is my best sexual experience I have ever had and honestly, I refuse to give it up. I refuse to give *her* up. She has brought the three of us together in a way none of us could have comprehended. She has never judged me and Hudson for our wants, she embraced them and made us feel supported and wanted without even trying.

Peyton was made for us.

"That was..." She laughs and the sound brings a smile to my face as I ease out of Hud and stand. "Everything," she breathes out. I stare at her in wonder. Van and Hudson are both looking at her as if they can sense the rightness of this as well. Hudson slowly eases out of her and steps back. She focuses down on Van and tentatively reaches out to grip the edge of his mask.

"Don't." That one word from him has her freezing.

"Why?" she whispers.

"You aren't ready for what happens after you know," he says in that deep tone he uses when we wear the masks. She hesitates for a second before withdrawing her hand, then slowly climbs off Van. She turns around and searches for her clothes. When she reaches for her jeans I snatch them from her.

"What are you doing?" she asks.

"We aren't finished with you, Bunny. We have all night and I plan to fuck every hole before you get to limp home." Her mouth pops open in surprise.

"You two gonna fuck again?" she asks, darting her gaze between me and Hudson. We both chuckle. I press against her and grip the back of her neck, forcing her onto her tiptoes as she holds my stare.

"Yeah, baby, we're gonna do it again *and* again and every time we do, we'll be thinking of you and how fucking perfect that pussy feels wrapped around our cocks. Now, get on your knees and clean me up." Hunger surges in her eyes. She eagerly obeys and drops to her knees before me, not knowing that my dick was just buried in her brother's ass makes this so much sweeter. She wraps her lips around me and moans. A strangled groan escapes me. I'll be hard in seconds and ready to take her again and again until the fucking sun rises and she is forced to limp her sexy ass out of these woods.

"Peyton!" I shout as we wait for her to get her ass downstairs. We didn't finish with her until dawn this morning. The guys and I stayed at the church last night in Van's office, there was no way we would be able to beat her home. When we got back this morning and saw the Easter basket we got her sitting on the counter, I choked on air while Van and Hudson laughed their asses off.

"I'm coming! Hang on," she hollers as we hear her running around upstairs. I know for a fact she will be sore today and it brings me great pleasure to know she will be thinking about all of us all day long. When she finally comes down the stairs, my eyes widen at the state of her. She's wearing gray sweats that hang low on her hips and a white crop top that exposes her toned stomach. Her hair is wet and loose around her shoulders and her eyes are bloodshot from lack of sleep. When she winces and limps toward the kitchen to grab her water bottle, I bite down on my cheek to keep from smiling. She stalks past Van and Hudson who are both trying not to laugh. We follow her out of the house and head next door to her mom and Ken's house, they are both waiting out front for us.

"Peyton, why do you look so wrung out?" her mother asks. Hudson starts coughing to mask his laughter. I turn away from them and greet Ken.

"I haven't been sleeping properly," she lies.

"Well, you need to take better care of yourself and your body. Like I have always told you—"

"Yes, I know, Mom. My body is my temple and I should cherish it. That is the way the Lord wanted us to think of ourselves." Sarcasm and annoyance is thick in her tone. Before her mother can irritate her more, I cut in and say hello. I have no idea why Van and Peyton had to accompany us today, but Hudson told us that his dad and Lenior wanted the four of us to come over.

Ken leads us through the house and points out the parts of the house that will need fixing. Between both mine and Hudson's schedules, this will be a slow build. I'm fully booked and Hudson has a shit load of projects going on at the moment.

"They said the plumbing could be finished within three to four weeks," Ken says. Hudson rubs the back of his neck and I know he hates having to be the asshole and tell his father it's gonna be a lot longer than that before they can move back into their home. I'll be honest, it doesn't bother me if it takes ten years because that means Peyton will still be with us.

"Dad, it's gonna be a few months before you and Lenior will be able to move back in." His father's face falls.

"If I can get the town to help pitch in, would that hurry the rebuild along?" Van asks us. Both Hudson and I share a look and nod.

"With us as the head of the build, I doubt they will want to pitch in," I admit.

Van's eyes darken. "You leave the town to me," he grits out.

"I was hoping we could have the house finished before Peyton leaves." All three of us swing our gazes toward the girl in question. She shoots her mother a glare.

"Thanks, Mom. I hadn't told them yet," she hisses. Lenior cringes and mutters an apology.

"What does she mean?" Hudson presses.

Pey nibbles on her bottom lip and drops her gaze to the floor. "I got accepted into Brown in the fall," she says quietly.

"You're leaving?" I whisper, hurt lacing my tone. She lifts her gaze to meet mine and I see guilt churning in the depths of those beautiful blue eyes I have come to love.

"I applied to Brown before I moved here. I..." She clamps her mouth closed and looks at each of us. She owes us nothing but yet she feels what we do, this unexplainable pull between the four of us. "I didn't think I would get accepted so I never mentioned it to anyone."

"That was why your father called?" Van hedges. She exhales and nods. "Good luck, have fun and all that shit," he bites out before stalking off. Peyton's shoulders slump and I know this must be hard for her, but it's worse for us. She has no idea we are the guys in the masks, we are the ones she is leaving behind. She may have started to feel for us and if she somehow knew the truth, maybe those feel-ings would be enough for her to stay.

"I gotta go," Hudson mutters then follows after Van.

She lifts those tear filled eyes to me and I crumble. I wrap my arms around her and hold her close. "We'll figure it out." I have no idea what I mean by that, but I just need her to know we are here and we are an option.

CHAPTER SEVENTEEN

PEYTON

After Hudson and Van took off, I ran home. I couldn't face any of them. I have no idea why I feel so guilty for leaving and going to college, but somewhere along the way I guess I... fell for all of them and now faced with this choice I don't know what to do. My phone vibrates again, drawing a sigh from me.

Saint - You're late.

Me - I'm not coming.

Goliath - Do you want to be punished?

Mac - You have ten minutes to move your ass.

I read the most recent message and shake my head.

Saint - Don't make me come to you.

Me - I'm tired.

When the three little dots don't appear I sigh in relief, the guys haven't come home and I don't blame them for being angry with me. I just wish my mom had kept her mouth shut and let me tell them. I snuggle into my bed and close my eyes, hoping that when I wake in the morning everything will be okay and they will give me a chance to explain. I hated seeing the crushed looks on each of their faces. It almost looked like I broke their hearts or something.

I jolt awake when a hand covers my mouth, my scream trapped as I fling my arms and try to fight, but the moment my eyes register the three glowing masks, I drop my arms back to my sides.

"You made us come to you," one of them growls.

Guilt gnaws away at my insides. I love how these three guys make me feel and how they allow me to embrace my sexuality, but somehow I've gone and caught feelings for three others. Now being with them feels like a betrayal to Hudson, Van and Kye. It's fucking crazy considering the guys have never outright said they have feelings for me but

I can just tell they feel something, and that shit has been playing on my mind daily.

"Now, we get to punish you," the one covering my mouth says. The hallway light casts a soft glow in my room, giving me my first real look at them without natural lighting as my guide. I push his hand off my mouth and run my gaze over each of them.

"This is the last time," I say quietly.

"This ends when *we* say it ends," the one at the end of my bed on the right growls. Call me crazy, but even with the masks I am starting to be able to tell them apart. Like, I know that it was Saint that just spoke. The one kneeling on the bed beside me is Goliath and the one beside Saint is Mac. They may wear the same glow in the dark rabbit masks and dress the same, but I can still somehow tell the difference between them. The three of them remind me of my guys and that's why this is harder than I want it to be. I can never have those three, but I can have these guys. Unfortunately all it will ever be with these three is sex and I need more than that.

I say nothing because this will end, I leave in a couple of weeks for Brown. They may be able to find me in this tiny town, but Rhode Island is too big to find one single person. When I leave this place, I'll be leaving these three and Van, Hud and Kye. Just the thought alone has my chest aching.

Mac leans forward and grips my sleep shorts. I don't

fight when he tugs them down my legs. Saint lifts my shirt and rids me of it. I lay here utterly exposed and at their mercy. I should kick them out so I don't risk the others hearing what is about to happen in my room.

"We can't be loud, the others—"

Goliath cuts me off. "The house is empty, you'll be screaming tonight and even if they were home we wouldn't give a fuck. You're ours and it's about time you and them learn that, because you belong to us, Peyton Jordan." His declaration sends a shiver down my spine, need unfurling in my belly at his claim.

Fuck it!

If this is going to be my last night with them, then I plan to make the most of it and enjoy every damn fucking second. I widen my legs for them so they can have a good view of my pussy. Their groans embolden me. I reach for Saint. He tenses when I lift his mask and grips my wrists, halting my movements.

"Blindfold me if you must tonight, but the three of you are going to let me taste those lips." Saint turns to the other two. The three of them seem unsure and this is my first time seeing them this way. Normally they are always in control and in charge but not tonight.

Tonight, I'm calling the shots and taking what the fuck I want from each of them.

Mac moves across my room and snatches a scarf that I had hung over my vanity. I sit up and wait for him to shield my eyes. The moment my vision turns black all my senses go on high alert. I feel Saint shuffling closer to me. I gasp when his hand grips the back of my neck, then a second later I feel his soft lips press against mine. I throw my arms around his neck and moan as he grants me entry into his mouth. The taste of him overwhelms me and short circuits my brain. Mac cups my tits, forcing me to arch into his hold, needing more. I gasp into Saint's mouth when I feel Mac lick a trail from my shoulder to my neck and suck on my tender flesh.

"Open those legs for me, Bunny," Goliath demands. I do as he says. He runs his hands along my legs, sending a shiver of anticipation through me. I blindly trail my hand down Saint's chest as I feel Goliath position himself between my legs. I grip Saint through his jeans. He breaks the kiss and groans. Mac grips my chin and forces me his way so he can claim my lips in a kiss filled with hunger. When Goliath swipes his tongue through my folds, I cry out and Mac swallows the sound.

Saint frees his cock, then guides my hand back to his shaft. Fuck, this is too much but at the same time it's not enough. I continue to pump Saint as I reach for Mac, only to find bare flesh beneath my hand.

He's naked!

I trail my fingers along his abs and relish in the feeling of his bare skin. I wrap my hand around his shaft, gripping him tight and hard, just how he likes it.

"Mac, on your back," Saint snarls. Mac breaks our kiss and does as he was ordered. I reach down between my legs and run my fingers through Goliath's hair, blindly holding him in place as Saint pulls out of my hold.

"Fuck," I moan when Goliath pushes his tongue inside my pussy. "Yes, taste me," I plead.

"Bring her here," Mac growls. Hands grip my waist and lift me. "Ride me," Mac barks as I'm positioned on his lap. I reach between us and blindly line him up with my entrance. I slowly sink down onto his cock and moan at the feeling of him sliding inside me. I'm still tender and sore from last night, but the pain mixed with the sensation of him inside me is a heady mix.

"Her ass is yours, brother," Saint says in that gravelly tone of his from beside me as Goliath comes up behind me. I cry out when he sinks his teeth into the tender flesh between my neck and shoulder. Mac grips my waist, holding me still as Goliath releases his bite and pushes me forward until I'm flat against Mac's chest. He parts my cheeks and I wait for the feeling of the lube, but to my utter fucking pleasure it isn't lube that circles my tight hole, it's his tongue.

Mac captures my lips in a heated kiss, swallowing all the sounds tumbling out of me as Goliath eats my ass. My body takes on a mind of its own and I can't stop it from grinding against Mac. Need is riding me hard. Before I can enjoy it more, Goliath pulls back and then presses the head of his cock against my hole and slowly eases inside me. My pussy clamps down on Mac. I push back, needing them both buried deep inside me. I rise until my back is flush against Goliath's chest, then swing my arm back to grip the back of his neck as I rest my head against his shoulder.

I wish I could see their faces.

"Fuck, baby, you look so good with their cocks inside you," Saint praises.

"I want the three of you at once," I plead.

"You heard our girl, brother, put that cock in her mouth," Goliath growls from behind me. Anticipation holds me in a chokehold as I wait for Saint to get in position. I'm jostled as he moves on the bed. I feel his legs move over each side of Mac, then the tip of his cock is brushing against my lips. I open without being prompted and suck him.

Goliath pulls back and slams inside me. I reach out and grip Saint's thighs to keep myself steady, while Mac and Goliath thrust inside me punishingly. Saint's thrusts are hurried and angry. They have never fucked me like this before. It slowly dawns on me that they are being so rough and aggressive because I defied them and made them come to me instead of obeying their orders.

Saint's fingers tangle in my hair and tug on the strands. "You swallow every fucking drop when I come," he growls. I moan around him in answer as the other two continue to slam inside me mercilessly. This unhinged side of them is fucking sexy. I love that they are losing control and giving into their baser needs. It's fucking hot and has me meeting them thrust for thrust, chasing my release, needing it more than my next breath. My cheeks hollow as I suck Saint deeper, trying to swallow all of him. Spit drips down my chin as I gag around him. The sound only seems to fuel them all. I scream around Saint when Mac slams inside my greedy little cunt, hitting that sweet spot. Goliath's thrusts turn hurried and deeper, pushing me right to the edge. I feel all three of them expanding inside me and I know they are all on the edge with me, ready to explode into oblivion and ride the fucking wave of pleasure.

Three more thrusts and then we are all falling. Stars explode into my vision as Saint comes down my throat. I choke but he doesn't release me when I try to pull back. Tears leak from my eyes as he forces me to swallow every fucking drop. Mac and Goliath still as aftershocks roll through me without constraint.

When I finally manage to swallow every drop, Saint releases his hold on my hair and his hand knocks my blindfold down. I blink rapidly, allowing my eyes to adjust for a second but the moment I do, everything inside me freezes.

"Fuck." I flick my eyes up only to be met with the sight of wide blue eyes that belong to my priest. I look down between his legs to find Kye's brown eyes staring directly at me. I take a deep breath and peer over my shoulder, locking eyes with my brother's bright green eyes, guilt swirling in the depths of those eyes.

They didn't angry fuck me because I disobeyed them, they did it because they are angry I'm leaving.

"Get. Out," I grit out through clenched teeth. Hurt flashes in Hudson's eyes as he slowly pulls out of me. The instant he does, I leap off Kye and run out of the room, locking myself in the bathroom down the hall.

We fucked up.

Oh, we fucked up so badly and there is no way to explain our actions. The three of us fell for her and allowed our want for her to overshadow everything. We should have come clean but we didn't. Kye and Hudson regret doing it but not me, I wouldn't change a single fucking thing because she was—*is* ours.

"What the fuck are we going to do?" Kye asks. We tried to coax Peyton out of the bathroom for over an hour but she refused. This morning we went to check on her only to find her room empty, all of her things were gone. Hudson rushed outside to check if her car was gone and it was. He called his stepmother to ask if she had seen Peyton. Lenior told him that Peyton had decided to head to Brown early to get set up. She wasn't happy that her daughter fled without saying goodbye, but the only hope we have is that Peyton promised to come back when the house was fixed.

I scrub a hand down my face. "Nothing." Both of them swing their gazes to me.

"The fuck does that mean?" Hudson snaps.

"It means what the fuck did we expect? You really think everyone in this damn fucking town will be cool with her fucking all three of us?" I shout. Both of their faces fall.

"I love her, man," Hudson admits, shocking me.

"Same," Kye mutters. I eye both of my best friends and shake my head. "Oh, so you're telling us you don't feel anything for her?" The angry lilt to Kye's tone has my shoulders falling.

"I took the collar off for her so what do you think, asshole?" I force out through clenched teeth.

"I feel... empty without her, man," Hud says quietly.

I sigh and nod my agreement. "Yeah, man, I get it. Shit doesn't feel right without her." Both of them grunt their agreement. Tired of feeling lost and hating not knowing what she's thinking, I pull my phone from my pocket. Both of the guys grin at me as if they know what I'm about to do.

Saint - You can run but you can't hide from us, Bunny.

Goliath - What he said…

Mac - Come home.

Mac - Please.

My breath hitches when I see she has read our messages. I wait for the three little dots to appear and don't realize I'm silently praying for her response until Hudson growls and storms out of the living room. It's been over an hour and she still hasn't replied. Defeat courses through me. I finally found the perfect girl who doesn't curse me for my urges, who forced me out of the prison I had locked myself in and now she's gone.

Three weeks later…

Today will be my last service. The town wasn't exactly happy when I announced that I would be resigning, but I no longer feel the calling I once did. I do have a calling, but it isn't to the man above. It's to a beautiful blonde in Rhode Island who has no idea we are all about to uproot our lives and chase her. Hudson, Kye and I all got together and managed to find a company to finish the remodeling on Ken and Lenior's home at a decent price. The town even offered to throw another fundraiser to help them out. Ever since she left, the guys and I have been lost.

Three days after she left, I told the guys I was leaving to go after her. Their reply was one I didn't expect. They both admitted to wanting to leave this place the second they realized she was gone, but they refused to leave without me. I had no idea they never left this town because of me, but they are my brothers and we stick together. I found solace in this place but now, it doesn't feel like home without her.

Hudson told his dad and Lenior the truth about what's happening between us and Peyton. Lenior lost her shit and refused to accept it. Ken just said he was disappointed. It wasn't the reaction we were hoping for but it still won't stop us from loving her. We all decided to ring her father before Lenior had the chance to spill the beans. It shocked the three of us to our core when he laughed and said he already knew. He proceeded to tell us that Peyton had admitted she had feelings for the three of us a few weeks back. He said he knew his daughter was too much for one man to handle. He was the one who gave us her address and told us to chase her because she is worth the risk. We couldn't agree more.

Hudson and Kye joined me today, knowing that I'd need their help to clear my office out after the service. I know for a fact Lenior has already run her mouth to the town about my relationship with her daughter. All morning I've been getting glares and quite a few people are missing from Sunday service. I wrap up and shake the hands of a few locals, Ken being the last one to come up to me. With a tight smile on his face, I hold my hand out to him. He looks over my shoulder and I know Kye and Hud are standing behind me. He sighs and places his hand in mine.

"I think you have one last confession to hold, Father." My brows draw together. "I think you may need... back up for this one." He shoots us all a weird look, then follows the others out the doors and closes them behind him, but not before flicking his gaze toward the confessional as if urging the three of us. When the doors close, I decide to play along. I open the door to the confessional, and both of the guys poke their heads in. The space is too small to fit all of us. I draw the partition open and my eyes widen instantly. Both Kye and Hudson go stiff at the sight.

"Forgive me, Father, for I have sinned." Her voice is like a balm to my dark soul.

I clear my throat and swallow audibly before I speak. "Would you like to confess your sins?" She slowly turns her head toward us, the sight of her beautiful face has my breath hitching. She looks between the three of us.

"I have had impure thoughts about my priest." I suck in a sharp inhale. "I've done unspeakable things with my stepbrother." Hudson groans and bites down on his fist to remain silent. "I enjoy watching my stepbrother and his best friend fuck, but I enjoy it more when they include me." Kye fucking whimpers. "Forgive me, Father, for I want to continue sinning with them." Kye darts next door and yanks her door open. She stares at him with a devilish smirk. "I haven't finished confessing my sins," she purrs.

Kye reaches out and cups her face between his hands. "Baby, God won't absolve you of your sins after the four of us defiled this very confessional." Laughter bursts out of her. Kye silences it when he smashes his lips against hers. Hudson and I both leap out of the confessional. Hud tugs back and helps Peyton out. She stares up at him with an unsure look in her eyes.

"You told my mom." It's not a question. Hud nods and grips her face between his hands.

"Yeah, baby, I want you and I don't give a fuck what anyone has to say about it." She pushes up onto her tiptoes and presses her lips against his. Hudson groans and jerks back. "You need to stop that or we will defile this church again." The three of them laugh. Peyton takes a deep breath, then slowly turns to face me.

"I want the man beneath the collar, no reservations. I need all of you." I smirk and move forward, then grip the back of her neck, forcing her into me as I bend down and skim my lips over hers.

"Bunny, you made me a *Dirty Priest* and now you have to deal with the aftermath of your creation. Now, get your ass into my office and bend over that desk. We have to punish you for leaving."

She scoffs. "You lied to me!"

"You took our pussy away," Hudson snarks.

"I can't," she mumbles.

"Why the hell not?" Kye snaps.

"I'm on my period," she mutters.

Laughter comes from the other two as I smile down at her. "Oh, baby, allow me to feast on the blood of Christ one last time in this place and mark you with the holy cross."

EPILOGUE
PEYTON

Six months later...

Brown is amazing. People here don't judge or even bat an eye at me with my guys. Tess even managed to escape that small ass town and got into Brown with me! The guys and I have an apartment off campus. Hudson has been so busy with projects since we moved here, and Kye managed to set himself up downtown and open another mechanic shop, which he loves. He gets way more money than he was making before and both of them seem so happy. Van, on the other hand, my dirty priest has decided he wants to invest. None of us knew that Van was loaded.

Apparently he comes from a wealthy family and even has two brothers and a dad that Hudson and Kye didn't know existed. He was the one to help fund Kye and Hudson's business here. He also just bought a hotel that he plans to revamp and open in the fall.

The move to Rhode Island has been the best thing for us. Ken still calls Hudson once a month but my mom has cut me off. I knew she wouldn't understand my relationship with the guys and that's okay. Dad on the other hand, he freaking loves them and is planning to come out here for another visit when he gets back.

I never thought that I would be so lucky to find a single amazing guy who enjoyed my... needs, but it turns out, I wasn't destined for one but three and they love me. They still bring out the masks every so often. My hunger for them hasn't lessened, even after all this time. They are still ravenous for me every night.

"So, when did you want to leave?" Tess asks from beside me.

"Van said it's like an eight hour drive to his father's cabin. I'm nervous to meet him and his brothers," I admit.

Tess snorts. "Girl, you will be fine."

"Easy for you to say!"

"Babe, I promise I won't be far behind. I'll be by your side the whole time and so will your guys." Her words ease some of the tension. Ever since Van told us about his dad inviting us out to their cabin I have been a nervous wreck. I'm so worried he won't like me. "Girl, I will be the odd one out, at least you have your guys with you." I cringe and shoot her a grateful smile. I practically forced Tess to come with us on this little trip because I needed my girl with me for moral support. I love my guys, but I can't bitch to them like I can with Tess.

"How is the dating app going?" I ask, changing the subject.

"Oh my God, I've been talking to this guy, he's a lot older and a single dad—"

"Bunny." I whirl around and smile at the sight of my guys leaning against the large tree in the middle of the quad.

Tess groans beside me. "Go on, I'll catch up with you tomorrow," she says. I mutter a quick goodbye and run to them. Kye catches me when I jump into his arms. His lips meet mine for a second before Hudson is ripping me away and kissing the air out of my lungs. Hud growls into my mouth when Van smacks the back of his head.

"Let my girl go, *Goliath*," Van snaps. I laugh and tug free of Hud's hold and step into Van.

"So demanding, *Saint*," I tease as I kiss him.

"Don't forget about *Mac Daddy*, baby," Kye adds. I shake my head and shoot Van a wink as I interlock my fingers with his and face them all.

"She's our girl, asshole," Hudson snaps. Van loves riling him up and refers to me as *his* just to piss Hudson off. Kye slings his arm around Hudson's shoulders and pulls him into his side.

"Do you need some one-on-one time with the Mac Daddy?" Kye purrs suggestively to Hudson. The raw sexual tension wafting between them has me clenching my thighs to try and dull the ache forming. I get so wet watching them fuck. Van loves it and always fucks me while I watch them. Don't get me wrong, I love having all three of them inside me but it's different when two of them are in me and Hudson or Kye are inside the other as they fuck me.

"You gonna suck me better?" Hudson asks with a pout, earning a snort from Van.

"Only if you ask nicely," Kye teases.

"Please, suck my cock," Hudson says in a husky tone that has me groaning and all of them swinging their gazes to me.

"What's wrong, baby?" Van whispers. I scowl at the asshole. He knows, and so do the other two, what their foreplay does to me and they fucking love it.

"We need to get home now. I don't have another class until this afternoon and I won't be able to focus until I have all of you." Van laughs.

"Homes so far away," he teases.

"I don't care," I bite out.

"There's a church down the road?" Van suggests with a wag of his brows.

"Dirty–fucking–priest," the three of us say in unison.

This, this right here is everything I could have wished for. I got them all and they have me. We are sinners. In our home, all Sinners are Welcome.

THANK YOU!

I think you all need to go and do at least a hundred hail
Mary's after reading this book!

Don't worry, I'll be doing them with you and praying the
good lord hasn't locked those pearly gates on me for good!
Thank you so much for taking a chance and reading Dirty
Priest, I am so in love with these four and the dynamic
they have. They were so easy to write and fucking fun!
Pey and her guys are destined for greatness and I believe
they got that in the end.

I cannot thank you enough for reading *Dirty Priest*, it
means the world to me that you have taken a chance on
reading one of my books!

ACKNOWLEDGMENTS

Marcus, my dirty sinner. This book is for you my daddy. That dick game is too fucking good and had me panting to write these fucking smut scenes!

MJ & Ray-Ray, my loves. I pray to God that you both never read this acknowledgment because that then means you read this book and fuck that. This book is not for you my darlings, please forgive mummy for being a dirty mofo!

Leah, my ride or die. Thank you for plotting this bitch with me and having my back, I couldn't do any of this without you my love!

My PA, Sarah–My Queen–Wilson, you make my job easy and keep the wheels turning while I write. None of this could happen without you, I am so in awe of you babe. I love you!

Alex Denver, the love of my fucking life, you are everything and more to me my darling. I love you beyond words.

My alpha's, Debbie, Clare, Erin and Samantha, all of you nasty bitches need to go to church and pray because ya'll are nasty and I fucking love it and love you for it.

My beta babes, Taay, Amber, Amanda, Nicole, Patti,

Morgan & Rizzo, I fucking love you crazy ladies. Thank you for sinning with me!

My ARC army girls, thank you beautiful souls so fucking much for always sticking by me and trusting me to mend those hearts that I break.

Lizz, you spoil the fuck out of me and I am so grateful to you for everything you have done and continue to do for me. None of this could be done without you babe and I love you so much.

My darling dark delicious readers, thank you again for following me and reading each of these books. I know I break your hearts and leave you mad when I end a book on a cliffy but I love that you trust me enough to heal those hearts and come back for more, I love you.

Sam xxx

<u>Fairytales With A Twist</u>
Condemned Beast
Secret Society/ Bully
Filthy Few
Forever Filthy
Filthiest Of Them All
Masked Men Novella (Pure Smut)
Dirty Priest
Dirty Daddy
Sports Romance
<u>Playing For Keeps</u>
Offside
Touchdown
End Game
Hail Mary
Blindside
RH Sports
Hate Us Like You Mean It
MM
Love Me Like You Mean It
Paranormal Romance
<u>The Veil Of Obsidian</u>
Of Time And Carnage
<u>The Dream Series</u>
A Beautiful Dream
A Twisted Fate
A Beautiful Nightmare
Redemption

Anarchy

<u>Brutal Savages</u>

Savage Lies

Brutal Truth

Savage Beast

Brutal Beauty

ABOUT THE AUTHOR

Samantha Barrett is originally from Auckland, New Zealand but living in Brisbane, Australia.

Sam writes all things dirty dark and delicious with a side of twisted mind fuck.

She is a lover of all things red flags and an anti-hero is a must.

www.ingramcontent.com/pod-product-compliance
Lightning Source LLC
Chambersburg PA
CBHW051705180726
48283CB00004B/1211

* 9 7 8 1 7 6 4 0 4 8 8 7 3 *